The Ruby of

Carminel

D1643152

To Luke Adam Saville

Also by Roger Mortimer
Eagle Warrior
Eagles' Revenge

The Ruby of Carminel

Roger Mortimer

EGMONT

First published in Great Britain 2002
by Egmont Books Limited
239 Kensington High Street
London W8 6SA

Text copyright © Roger Mortimer
Cover design copyright © 2002 Lee Gibbons

The moral rights of the author and the cover illustrator
have been asserted

ISBN 0 7497 4638 6

10 9 8 7 6 5 4 3 2 1

A CIP catalogue record for this title
is available from the British Library

Typeset by Avon DataSet Ltd,
Bidford on Avon, Warwickshire
Printed and bound in Great Britain
by Cox & Wyman Ltd, Reading, Berkshire

CONTENTS

Part Three: The Castle in the Clouds

Prologue:
The Black Widow Spider
of Salamex

'Bring me the Great Ruby of Power from Carminel!'

The spider's voice rose scarcely above a whisper. But her great web trembled at her power and in the pit that yawned beneath its golden threads, the sacred viper stirred uneasily.

'Did you hear me, Malatesta?'

'I heard you, Majesty.' Malatesta was a stoat,

commander of the elite Ermine Guard. So, he thought, it had come at last; Empress Ravanola, the great Black Widow Spider, ruler of the mighty empire of Salamex, was playing the opening move in her war against the Mouse Kingdom of Carminel. And in that war, there would be rich plunder for the stoats who fought in the empress's army, for the sea-rats who sailed her warships and for the vultures who fought in the skies. But for the Ermine Guard, and for its commander, there would be the richest plunder of all!

'The King of Carminel is only a child,' murmured Ravanola. 'But he is protected by the ruby's magic powers. Others have tried to conquer the Mouse Kingdom and have failed. But once I have the ruby, Carminel will be at my mercy.'

'It shall be done. How many ships may I take?'

'Enough to scare those miserable mice to death! Leave most of our fleet behind, they will be needed for the invasion. Sail into the harbour of Aramon, the capital of Carminel, and do plenty of damage!' The empress's laugh set her web quivering again and the viper hissed softly. 'But your attack will be merely a diversion. Under cover of the raid, you will lead your Ermine Guards ashore. Wait for darkness. Then sneak into the city and take the ruby. You will find it in the Great Cathedral, where these foolish mice have it on display for anyone to steal! When I have it, our vultures and our ships will attack Aramon, and all Carminel will be mine!'

Malatesta bowed, and was about to leave the throne-room when Ravanola called him back. 'Wait! I want you to take Gweir.'

Malatesta curled his lip in disgust. 'That stinking stoat?'

'He is no ordinary stoat!' Ravanola's sudden roar of anger made even the spiders of her bodyguard tremble. 'He is my magician, with power from the Snake-god who dwells far beneath my palace! Sneer at him at your peril, Lord Malatesta. He will be useful. Now go!'

Malatesta was not afraid of the empress. But he was not such a fool as to argue with her in her angry mood.

Leaving the throne-room, Malatesta passed through three archways, each guarded by a spider of the empress's bodyguard. As he entered the garden, the blistering summer sun struck him, and he hurried to the gatehouse, pausing a few minutes in its cool shadow. Then, he crossed the drawbridge which spanned the deep, dry moat that encircled Ravanola's palace: the House of the Snake.

Before him, the city of Kalamaris fell steeply away in a maze of narrow, twisting alleys, the over-crowded houses stinking in the burning heat. Malatesta hurried down to the harbour, where white-cloaked stoats of his elite Ermine Guard were waiting to row him out to his ship, the *Night Crow*. They had to help him into the boat, for one of Malatesta's paws was missing, hacked off in a battle long ago. In its place was a gleaming spike. The stoats took care to avoid it, for it was smeared with venom from the sacred viper; the slightest scratch meant death.

Once aboard, Malatesta summoned Captain Blacktail, his second in command. 'Send a message to the Port of Viperium. Twelve warships of the fleet must be sailed here at once. And summon my special squad.'

'You mean the Dirty Tricks bunch? Very good, my lord.'

Giving orders that he must not be disturbed, Malatesta shut himself in the *Night Crow*'s great cabin and planned his attack on Aramon. Since the Empress insisted, he would have to make use of Gweir. But the tall magician with the piercing eyes had the ability to see into other creatures' minds, something which Malatesta found distinctly uncomfortable.

An hour later, his plan of action complete, Malatesta threw back his head and laughed. Carminel was doomed, for if all went well, the mice would not even know that their ruby was gone until it was too late.

PART ONE
THE RUBY OF POWER

1 Black sails

'A plague on this infernal mist! I can hardly see my paw in front of my face.' Lukas, Bosun of the *Avenger*, heaved his powerful bulk up the ladder to the quarter-deck. 'D' you hear anything, skipper?'

Captain Roamer stood motionless, one paw resting lightly on the ship's wheel, his keen ears questing the mist. 'Yes. Listen.'

At first, Lukas could hear nothing. But suddenly, he caught the faint groaning of another ship's timbers and the creaking of ropes. 'Is it the *Raven*?' he whispered.

All day, the buccaneers had been chasing the great treasure-ship, homeward bound for Ravanola's Empire. The *Avenger* had almost caught her when the *Raven* had vanished into one of the sea mists that sometimes descended without warning in the great Southern Ocean. Roamer had followed, and was now wishing he hadn't.

'It might be the *Raven*. But there's more than one ship out there.'

Though the *Avenger*'s sails hung motionless, the ship was moving. 'We must be close to the island,' Lukas said softly. 'The tide's carryin' us towards it.'

The island was the buccaneers' hideaway, complete with fresh water and a golden, palm-fringed beach. Roamer was afraid that in the mist the *Avenger* might run aground; but until he knew what other ships were nearby, he dared not risk the noisy business of dropping the anchor.

'They're closer,' he whispered. 'Here they come!'

On the main deck, the silent sea-mice crouched like statues. Suddenly, they heard the dreadful sound of crying and wailing and a ghostly ship with black sails loomed out of the mist. The mice caught only a glimpse before it vanished. But another ship came gliding by and it, too, had black sails.

'Salamex pirates,' whispered Roamer, 'moving

faster than we are. They must be closer inshore, and there may be others.'

'But that terrible cryin'!' hissed Lukas. 'What did it mean?'

'Don't know. But there's nothing we can do . . . yet.'

For an hour, the *Avenger* crept silently through the mist. At last, a wind parted the white curtain and there lay the island, sunlit and inviting, half a mile to starboard. Cheesemite, the lookout, scampered up the rigging to the crosstrees near the top of the mainmast. But the black-sailed ships had vanished.

'No sign of the *Raven*, either!' called Cheesemite.

'That's a fortune gone west,' muttered Lukas.

Although the Empress Ravanola was now plotting against the Mouse Kingdom, for many years there had been peace between her Empire and Carminel. But in the great Southern Ocean there was ceaseless war, for there lay the Golden Islands, yielding gold, silver, spices and gems. The power-hungry Ravanola claimed these islands for herself. She barred merchants of Carminel from trading with the islanders, the peace-loving tamarins: small, nimble tree-dwellers, with golden fur and long tails. But the empress's treasure-ships were in constant danger from Carminel buccaneers; and no ship was swifter or better armed than the *Avenger* and no captain more daring than Roamer.

'Lukas, steer for Coriander Island. That crying we heard might have been tamarins. If the Black Widow's sea-rats have been taking prisoners, Chief Tia-roa will know of it.'

Leaving their island basking in the sunshine, the sea-mice sailed south for Coriander, one of the many islands where the tamarins lived. Buccaneers such as Roamer gave a fair price for their treasures: Ravanola's sea-rats simply helped themselves.

'Deck, there!' cried Cheesemite. 'Smoke on the southern horizon!'

'Make more sail!' snapped Roamer. Canvas thundered down, and as it caught the wind *Avenger* powered across the waves. As she drew near to the island, the scent of spices, carried on the wind, was almost swamped by the stench of burning.

The last of the sun was gilding the sails as the sea-mice dropped anchor in Coriander Bay. Of the tree-house settlement, nothing remained but smouldering heaps of ash and the little landing-stage had been hacked to pieces.

'Lower the boats,' said Roamer.

Beneath its pall of smoke, the darkening beach was deserted. But as the buccaneers crossed the sand towards the palm trees, Roamer caught a sudden movement in the undergrowth. 'This is Captain Roamer of the *Avenger*! Come out!'

The leaves parted and out crept a tamarin child. His golden fur was singed and his eyes were bright with tears. For a moment he stared at the tall buccaneer. Then, with a cry of relief, he ran towards him.

From all around the beach, other tamarins crept from cover. Recognising Chief Tia-roa, Roamer asked: 'Who has done this?'

'Who else but sea-rats?' said the chief bitterly. 'They burnt our houses, destroyed our crops. We hadn't enough gold to satisfy them, so they took twelve of our children to sell as slaves. Among them was my daughter.'

'Princess Tamina? Don't worry, old friend. We'll get them back.'

'There is more! These pirates were boasting that the Ermine Guard commander, Lord Malatesta, may his name be accursed, will soon sail for Carminel. He will do to Aramon what these vermin have done to us.'

'We'd best sail home and warn King Caladon,' said Lukas. 'But first, we must rescue these young tamarins. Give the sea-rats a taste of their own medicine, eh skipper?' he added with a grin.

Roamer grinned back. 'Yes! Tia-roa, we saw two pirate ships. Which one carried the prisoners?'

'The larger of the two. Her name is the *Vulture*.'

Roamer's mice shuddered at the name. The vultures who lived on the burning plains of Salamex were renowned for their cruelty. Roamer knew that if Ravanola were planning an invasion of Carminel, the vultures would certainly be a part of it. Sensing his crew's fear, he smiled. '*Avenger* will clip this vulture's wings! We'll leave a dozen sea-mice here to defend the island in case of another raid, and to help Tia-roa's tamarins rebuild their homes. The rest, back to the ship! We sail at once!'

2 The Vulture

'Deck, there! Land ahead!'

As Cheesemite's excited voice pealed down from the crosstrees, Roamer swung himself into the foremast rigging and stared into the gathering darkness. On the horizon, twinkling lights marked the position of Kalamaris, capital of Ravanola's Empire.

'Heave to!' Mice sprang to take in the sails, Lukas spun the wheel, the ship turned into the wind and wallowed to a standstill.

In the great cabin, Roamer and Lukas studied the

chart. 'See those cliffs that guard the harbour?' said
Roamer. 'We'll wait until it's completely dark, then
we'll steer for the eastern side; there's a bay that
should give us shelter from the wind and hide us
from any passing ship or patrol boat. From there,
you'll take a landing party ashore. Find the *Vulture*.
Then we'll launch the cutter and go in.'

An hour later, *Avenger* crept towards the land. The
sky was overcast; Roamer had only the harbour
lights to guide him as he steered for the eastern bay.
The wind was strengthening, whipping the waves
into white-caps. But as the ship rounded the tall
cliff, the wind died. Roamer dropped anchor in a
small, sheltered bay and the landing-party slipped
ashore.

Two hours later, a grim-faced Lukas followed his
sea-mice back aboard *Avenger*. 'Chief Tia-roa was
right about Malatesta's plans! We counted twelve
warships strung out across the harbour, takin' on
stores an' weapons. The place is crawlin' with
rowboats, goin' from one ship to another.'

'Where's the *Vulture*?'

'Lyin' at anchor on the western side of the
harbour. To reach her, our cutter will have to pass
through the middle of Malatesta's fleet! An' now it's
rainin',' he added, glaring at the sky.

'Just what we needed!' grinned Roamer. He turned to his raiding party. 'Lower the cutter. Leave the mast down. Four of you, take the oars. The rest, hide yourselves, the weapons and the barrel of gunpowder under the tarpaulin. I'll take the tiller. We'll disguise ourselves as one of these boats carrying stores; what more natural than to protect cargo from the rain by covering it with a tarpaulin? Give us an hour, Lukas, then take the ship to the harbour mouth and wait for us. Have the guns loaded and run out – just in case!'

As the cutter left the shelter of the bay and rounded the headland, the mice had to bend their backs and row hard against the blustering wind. At the tiller, Roamer narrowed his eyes against the spray, seeing the great ships lying at anchor and the swarms of small boats clustering around them. As the cutter entered the harbour, the wind blew less violently and Roamer steered boldly for the ships. Somewhere beyond them lay the *Vulture*.

Well disguised in capes and woollen caps, the sea-mice rowed through the midst of Malatesta's fleet. All round them, sea-rats were rowing boats laden with cannonballs and barrels of gunpowder. Some boat crews waved to the buccaneers, calling out cheerily about the dirty weather, and a ship's captain called to Roamer, demanding to know whether he had brought his ammunition. But Roamer shook his head and pointed to another warship and the rat cursed him and returned to his cabin.

At last, the cutter was clear of the fleet. 'Lie down!' hissed Roamer to the mice concealed beneath the tarpaulin. 'Make it look as if we've delivered our cargo!'

Suddenly, he tensed. The rain had stopped, the clouds had parted, and in the starlight Roamer saw two ships at anchor, the larger one lying closer to the harbour mouth. Roamer steered the cutter towards the larger ship's stern. Crossing it at a safe distance, he could just make out its name: *Vulture*.

'Rest oars,' he whispered. Gratefully, the tired crew obeyed, and Roamer let the cutter drift a little before pointing its bows towards the *Vulture's* port side.

'Out you come!' The sea-mice heaved back the tarpaulin, gratefully gulping in the fresh air as they passed round the pistols and cutlasses. Four of the mice who had lain hidden took over the oars; the rest crouched low.

'Ready, lads?' Twelve faces grinned back at him in the darkness. 'Then let's go!'

As the mice rowed steadily towards the *Vulture*, Roamer scanned the rigging of both pirate ships for lookouts. But he saw none and, as they drew closer, the shouting and laughter from both vessels reassured him. 'They're having parties in the stern cabins,' he whispered. 'With any luck, they'll be drunk by now! We're close enough. Ship oars!' The mice stopped rowing and Roamer allowed the cutter to drift alongside the *Vulture* until it was level with her bows. 'Now, Ben, up with the chain.'

'Roight, zur!' Bracing his feet on the deck, old Ben spat on his paws, then swung the chain. The others held their breath. This was the trickiest part of the expedition. But Ben had done this many times before and the chain caught on one of several mooring-hooks fastened to the *Vulture*'s bows. Roamer glanced anxiously towards the stern of the second ship. It was perilously close, its cabin windows ablaze with lights and the shouts of laughter louder than ever. Fortunately, none of the windows was open; all were well and truly misted up. But it only needed a sea-rat to feel like some fresh air . . .

'Up you goes, zur!' whispered Ben. Roamer clambered up the chain, hooked his paw across the bows and peeped over. A swift glance showed him that the beak-head, the narrow platform at the very front of the ship, was deserted. He swung himself aboard and reached out his paw to the next mouse in the line.

Soon, eleven mice were gathered on the beak-head; one had been left behind to guard the cutter and to give the alarm should it be spotted. In front of them loomed the fo'c'sle, the cabin at the front of the ship. Gently, Roamer eased open the door. Though the cabin stank of sea-rat, it was empty, and the door at the other end, leading to the main deck, was closed. In the faint light, Roamer could just see the outline of a hatch-cover.

'Open that.'

'Oi got'n, zur,' whispered Ben. He heaved up the hatch-cover, revealing a shadowy flight of steps, leading down into utter darkness.

'Light the lantern,' said Roamer. 'Now, follow me!'

3 Princess Tamina

Following the lantern's ghostly glimmer, the sea-mice crept between the lines of cannon. As they drew near to the stern, the din from the cabin above grew louder. At last, Roamer stopped before a stout, padlocked door. From behind it, the sea-mice could faintly hear the whimpering of the young tamarins.

Passing the lantern to Ben, Roamer levered off the padlock with his knife and flung open the door. Several little tamarins stared at him, wide-eyed with terror. Suddenly, a tiny dagger flew over his head and stuck, quivering, in the beam behind him and a tawny figure hurled itself at his throat, kicking and tearing with its long claws.

'Princess Tamina! Stop it! It's me, Roamer!'

The tamarin stopped trying to kill him and stared wide-eyed. 'Roamer! It's so dark I didn't recognise you. I thought you were one of the pirates! I hope I didn't hurt you too much!'

'No, but save your claws for the sea-rats! Now, the cutter's waiting, so if you and these youngsters are quite ready . . .?'

'I think so,' grinned Tamina. 'This cabin's disgusting; not at all what I'm used to!'

She pulled out her dagger, returning it to its hiding-place in her left boot. Then, shooing the children in front of her, Tamina followed the buccaneers. Silently, they clambered to the fo'c'sle, and onto the beak-head. Breathless with excitement, the little tamarins swarmed down the chain into the cutter. At last, only Roamer, Ben and the princess were left.

'Pass up that powder keg!' called Roamer softly. 'Now, Ben, you know what to do.'

'Aye, aye, sir!' Clutching the keg, and chuckling softly to himself, the old sea-mouse descended the ladder. 'What's he going to do?' asked Tamina.

'Blow up the ship. But there should be time for us to get clear first.'

The racket from the stern cabin was deafening as the party reached its height. Roamer was imagining Ben groping like a mole to the lowest deck, wedging the powder keg among the creaking timbers, laying the trail of gunpowder . . . A faint glow shone through the darkness followed by a distant sizzling. Minutes later, Ben's snout popped out of the hatch. 'All done, zur; 'er should blow in 'bout . . . oh, let's see now . . . say . . . four, five minutes.'

'Good work, Ben,' said Roamer. 'I remember the last pirate ship you blew up. That time, it was more like three minutes. Something the matter, Princess?'

'Not at all,' said Tamina, her voice shaking slightly. 'But perhaps we could talk in the cutter rather than on top of a powder keg?'

With Roamer at the tiller, the cutter swung away from the doomed ship. As they rounded the stern, where three great lanterns burned above the brightly-lit cabin, Roamer drew his double-barrelled pistol and fired a bullet through the windows.

Shocked silence; then, uproar! Windows flew open, sea-rats poked out their heads, all shouting at once, and Roamer bellowed: 'This is Captain Roamer of the *Avenger*! You have about two minutes to abandon ship before she's blown out of the water!'

A hulking rat in a gaudy uniform thrust his snout through the window. 'You're the ones wot are goin' to get blown up!' he yelled, and fired at the cutter. 'That's the captain,' muttered Tamina. Snatching Ben's pistol, she clawed back the hammer and fired.

'You'm missed him, Princess,' said Ben.

Tamina smiled grimly. 'He's dead.'

For a moment longer, the pirate captain stood motionless; then, he toppled into the water. 'He insulted me,' said Tamina, as the buccaneers cheered, 'and frightened the children half to death. I warned him what I'd do, if ever I had the chance.'

Though most of the pirates were leaping for their lives into the sea, some were still firing. Ben, who was staring with admiration at Tamina, suddenly fell with a squeal of pain, a bullet through his leg. Instantly, the princess knelt beside him, ripping her shirt to make a rough bandage while the other sea-mice fired back.

Suddenly, a streak of fire leapt from the *Vulture's* bows. A moment later, there came a deafening roar, smoke and flames billowed from the fo'c'sle, and, as more terrified rats hurled themselves into the sea, the whole ship lurched forward. The sea-mice cheered as the masts groaned and toppled and the stern rose into the air. For a moment, the ship hung motionless before plunging beneath the waves.

The sound of the explosion was still echoing across the water when lights sprang up in Malatesta's fleet and hundreds of voices started yelling at once. 'Time to go,' grinned Roamer. 'Hoist the sail!'

The cutter leapt forward, and Roamer steered boldly for a gap between two warships, laughing at the angry shouts and yells that followed the cutter's impudent dash. 'They won't fire! They'll only hit each other!'

From the deck of the *Night Crow*, Malatesta was screaming with fury. 'Up anchor, you miserable cowards! Sink that accursed boat!' But by the time the anchor was free, Roamer was almost clear of the harbour, heading for the welcome sight of the *Avenger* and her wildly cheering crew.

'What now, skipper?' grinned Lukas. The children were safely stowed away below decks, and Tamina was putting a clean bandage on Ben's wound. 'Back to the harbour and do some damage?'

Roamer was tempted, but . . . 'Not safe for the youngsters. Only needs one unlucky shot to hit us. Make sail! We'll return these tamarins to Coriander, then it's home to Aramon. We must warn King Caladon that Malatesta's on his way.'

The following evening, as the setting sun turned

the sea to gold, the *Avenger* dropped anchor in Coriander Bay and Roamer and four of the crew rowed the children ashore. The little tamarins squealed with delight as their parents rushed to meet them and Chief Tia-roa hugged his daughter and wept for joy. But his happiness was to be short-lived.

'Now, father, don't get carried away. Roamer's sailing for Aramon, and I'm going too.'

'Oh no you're not!' Roamer had been half-expecting this.

'Oh yes I am! I can shoot straight, and I'm a good nurse. What's more, the crew would like me to come.'

Roamer knew this was nonsense. A female aboard meant bad luck, as every sea-mouse knew. But to his astonishment, his mice were nodding and grinning at the princess. He scowled at her. 'What have you been saying to them?'

Tamina lowered her eyes. 'Is it my fault I'm popular?'

Spoilt, more like, thought Roamer grimly. But he had to admit that she had shown courage during the rescue and that Ben owed his leg, if not his life, to her prompt and skilful doctoring. Chief Tia-roa gave a rueful shrug, as if to say: what's the use? She'll get her own way, whether we like it or not!

'Oh, very well,' sighed Roamer. 'But if I –'

'Captain!' From the *Avenger*, Cheesemite's voice came floating across the water. *'Enemy fleet in sight!'*

4 Night attack

If Roamer hoped that Tamina might be put off by the prospect of battle, he was much mistaken! Once aboard, the Princess disappeared below decks, to re-emerge minutes later dressed in sailor's shirt and breeches, a cutlass at her side and a brace of pistols in her belt. Below her broad-brimmed hat, her long mane spread in a golden wave. The buccaneers gave her a cheer, convinced she would bring them nothing but good fortune, and Tamina beamed with pleasure at all the attention she was getting.

As darkness engulfed the island, *Avenger* slipped out

of the bay, sailing swiftly in pursuit of Malatesta's black-sailed fleet. For an hour or more, she skimmed over the starlit ocean until Cheesemite called from the crosstrees: 'Deck, there! Strange sail ahead, going slow! Rest of the fleet's *way* ahead!'

'This straggler might've sprung a leak,' said Roamer.

Or it may be a trap, thought Lukas. But Roamer shouted: 'Clear for action! Put out the lanterns! Princess, go below and await the wounded – *and don't argue!* Lukas, tell the lower deck gun-crews to load with double shot. Guns on the main deck to load with chainshot; that should bring their masts down if it comes to a fight!' Roamer's well-drilled crew leapt to obey and within minutes, *Avenger* was ready for battle.

Roamer was watching the enemy ship. 'She's not showing any lights, not even a stern-lantern. Lay us on a parallel course, Lukas. We'll keep our distance and let them fire first.'

Tensely, silently, the crew waited. *Avenger* drew closer. At Roamer's command, mice at the yard-arms smartly furled the topsails, until their ship was moving as slowly as the other. Leaning over the port-side rail, Roamer stared through his telescope. 'No sign of life. Can't even see anyone at the wheel...'

'Skipper! Look out!'

The enemy's gunports had flown open. A second later, all her cannons roared at once in a deafening broadside and smoke billowed as high as the masthead. But *Avenger* was barely in range. One or two shots struck her side, the rest fell short. Roamer laughed.

'He's fired too soon! Shake out the sails! Steer for their bows! Port-side gun-crews, stand by!'

Avenger tore down upon the other ship, and as the two vessels drew together like an arrowhead, Roamer yelled: '*Fire!*'

With a thunderous roar, *Avenger*'s guns hurled their deadly cargo across the narrow strip of water. The enemy ship reeled as double shots hammered her hull and, as chainshot screamed through her rigging, the foremast toppled, bringing down black sails like shrouds.

'Well done, lads!' cried Roamer. 'Hold your course, Lukas! Straight for her bows!'

The crew's cheering died away. *Avenger* was drawing perilously close, the long bowsprit with its single sail pointing from her bows like a spear at the enemy ship.

'Skipper . . .'

'Hold your course,' said Roamer calmly. 'Our

broadside must have done some damage, or they'd have fired by now. If they force a crash, we'll board them. But they won't. There! What did I tell you!'

At the last second, the sea-rat captain's nerve had broken. With black sails trailing over the side, his ship swung clumsily away. 'Take in mainsails!' yelled Roamer. 'Now, swing her to port! We'll cross behind and rake her from end to end!'

Lukas spun the wheel, turning the ship until her bows were pointing at the enemy's stern. The sea-rats fired a ragged broadside. Too late! A few shots screamed through *Avenger*'s rigging; the rest flew harmlessly past to splash into the sea.

'Starboard gun-crews, your turn!' yelled Roamer. 'Fire as we cross her!'

As she sailed behind the enemy ship, *Avenger*'s guns erupted in smoke and flame. Lukas imagined the terrible destruction as roundshot smashed through the stern and flew the whole length of the ship.

The last gun roared, and Roamer brought *Avenger* round on a course parallel with the enemy, this time with those black sails to starboard. 'Re-load!' yelled Roamer, but already his gunners were ramming in powder and shot, fearful of the broadside that must surely come.

But the other ship remained silent. 'That attack on her stern finished her,' said Roamer. 'Look! She's settling in the water! She's keeling over!'

High in the crosstrees, Cheesemite had been so absorbed in the battle that he had not noticed that danger was rapidly approaching. Fortunately, Princess Tamina, bored with waiting below, chose that moment to appear on deck, determined to join in the excitement. She was heading for the quarterdeck, when a movement out at sea caught her eye. 'Look out! Another of those black-sailed beasts! Attacking from the left! I mean *port*!'

The ship looked enormous. The big creamy bow-wave, just visible in the starlight, and the tower of billowing black sail showed how swiftly she was approaching. 'Time to go, Skipper?' asked Lukas nervously.

'Steady, Lukas, there's plenty of time. Thank you, Princess. Now get below, *if* you please!'

Tamina drew breath to argue; but such was Roamer's authority that for once she meekly obeyed. Besides, this new ship would be a tough enemy. There might well be wounded sea-mice for her to look after.

If Tamina was worried, the buccaneers were aghast; the massive ship bearing down on them seemed to fill the ocean. But Roamer was carefully gauging its speed. 'Port-side guns, *fire!*' Instantly, *Avenger*'s guns roared. The big ship was close enough for the buccaneers to see gaping holes appear in her sails and a mass of splinters fly from her bows.

'Stand by aloft!' snapped Roamer. 'Set all sails . . . wait for it . . . *Now*!'

Sails thundered down, billowed in the wind, *Avenger* leapt clear and Cheesemite squealed: 'Cor, look at *that*!'

Until her sudden movement, *Avenger* had been concealing her beaten foe from the swiftly-moving enemy ship. Now the other captain saw his peril: a floating wreck lying directly across his bows.

Lukas imagined the panic, saw the great ship frantically trying to swing clear of the danger. But it was too late. With a rending crash, the oncoming ship ploughed into the wreck, so violently that her foremast was torn from its base and the buccaneers cheered as the mainmast collapsed as well.

'Two down, ten to go!' yelled Roamer. His mice cheered themselves hoarse. Not one of them doubted that their Captain could take on the whole of that sinister fleet and destroy them all.

'Deck, there!' cried Cheesemite. 'Enemy fleet's turning back!'

'They'll be picking up survivors,' said Roamer. 'A pity there wasn't time for us to do that; we might've learned something about Malatesta's battle plans. Now, we must overtake his ships, sail fast to Aramon and warn the King. Lukas, tell the cook to serve hot food to the crew – and a double ration of rum! I'm going to my cabin to look at the chart.'

But before Roamer could leave the quarterdeck, Rio, the ship's stout carpenter, came panting up from below. 'Capitano! You ain't gonna like this, but Rio, he gotta tell you. That devil-ship, he done us some damage.'

'How bad is it?' asked Roamer calmly.

Rio spread his paws wide. 'Beeg hole, slap on the bows! Is above waterline, but only just. The worst place if you wanna chase them devils!'

'So every time the ship dips into a trough –'

'We ships many water! I already patch de hole with sail-cloth, but that no stoppa the water, she still seep in, ya know? We gotta the pumps a-goin', so we no sink. But you wanna Rio to repair it, we need to keep the ship still. For much hours. Then we gotta slap on pitch an' tar, an' –'

'So much for a fast voyage to Carminel!' exclaimed Lukas bitterly. 'We'll have to creep along like an old tub.'

'Rio, do the best you can,' said Roamer. 'Lukas, take in sail! Keep the ship in darkness. We'll steer north–east and hold that course for an hour; we must keep clear of the enemy. After that, I'll lay a course for Carminel. We'll not be able to overtake Malatesta's fleet, and until that hole's patched we can't fight them. We'll just have to shadow them. But when they attack Aramon, then we must fight them, leak or no leak!'

5 Malatesta strikes

The first day of the great Aramon Market dawned bright and clear. Beneath shady trees in the Great Cathedral Square, where brightly-coloured awnings fluttered in the breeze, dozens of traders were crying their wares. Country-mice from the outlying farms were busily slicing rounds of cheese, setting out jugs of buttermilk and offering pats of butter wrapped in dock leaves. From the High Collada Mountains, the Kingdom of the Eagles, came beavers, their huge front teeth set in a permanent, good-natured grin. They were selling fat salmon and slithery eels, packed in ice that was already melting in the autumn sunshine. It was a cheerful, bustling scene, with no hint of the terrors to come.

Old Cardinal Matthias moved slowly through the busy crowds. Mice doffed their caps to him and their wives dropped curtsies. Not just because he was Chief Priest of the Lord of Light; all Aramon loved the grey-furred cardinal for his goodness, and his kindness to the city's poor. Mother Bibo, his cook-housekeeper, followed him through the market, peering short-sightedly through her spectacles, her basket in one paw, her purse in the other.

As usual, a crowd of children thronged round the kindly cardinal. Most were homeless orphans who lived on the streets, but their leader was a chubby little mouse called Cranberry, whose father owned the famous 'King's Head' tavern in Vittles Lane. 'Look, yer 'oliness!' he squeaked. 'Salmon!'

Cardinal Matthias' eyes sparkled. 'Now, that is a treat! Mother Bibo, would you kindly purchase one – no, let's enjoy ourselves – *two* fat salmon!'

Mother Bibo smiled to herself as she counted out the pennies. The cardinal ate little, his usual dinner consisting of a dish of lentils and a morsel of dry bread. But once a year, at market time, with so much delicious food on sale, old Matthias liked to treat not only himself, but also his cook and the many poor orphans who came to his house for meals and were never turned away.

While Mother Bibo added the salmon to the Valladale cheese and Barrowdown butter already in her basket, the cardinal spoke quietly to Casey, the chief beaver. 'What news from the mountains?'

'Why, ever'thing's just fine an' dandy, Cardinal,' said Casey in his broad mountain accent. 'Young Aquila the eagle, Hyperion's son, y'know, he's almost fully grown.'

'And my old friend, Marengo?'

Lord Marengo was chief of the hardy tribe of mice who had lived with the eagles in the High Collada Mountains since the days of Gideon, the great Eagle Warrior. 'He's just fine,' said Casey. 'Not so young as he used to be; in fact, he's gettin' kinda old. But his eye's bright as ever, and he can still use a sword an' fire a pistol like a young warrior.'

'I'm glad to hear it. One of these days, we may have need of him and his eagles.' The cardinal was thinking of the young King Caladon. Not yet fully grown, he would make a fine king one day, if only . . .

Casey guessed what the cardinal was thinking. 'Is Duke Flambeau still keepin' young Caladon down?'

Flambeau! The king's vain, ambitious uncle – the Red Duke of Aramon! The cardinal sank his voice to a whisper. 'I fear that he is. The Lord of Light knows, I try to see the good in all mice; but there is little good in that overmighty duke!'

From the *Night Crow*'s quarterdeck, out in the bay, Malatesta was studying the harbour through his telescope. Beyond the cluster of ships moored at the quayside, the waterfront seemed almost deserted. There were no defences; even the battlements of the Great Fortress, high on its rock away to the right, were bare of guns. Malatesta shut his telescope. 'Soft as a plum,' he murmured. He raised his paw, the spike flashed in the sunlight, and, as the signal-gun banged out, two of his ships weighed anchor and sailed slowly into the harbour.

With a roar of cannon-fire, Malatesta's ships blasted the little waterfront houses to matchwood. In Cathedral Square, there was a moment of stunned silence; then, as another roar echoed across the city, the crowd dissolved in panic. Yelling and screaming, they tried to get out of the square, but the lanes were so narrow that they were soon jammed with squealing mice.

'Go home, children, all of you!' The cardinal

spoke with such authority that the young mice darted off. Most lived in the slums by the North Gate, and were soon worming their way through the crowd. But Cranberry's home was in Vittles Lane, close to the docks.

'The firing's comin' from the 'arbour!' he squeaked excitedly. 'I'm goin' to see what's 'appenin'!'

'Cranberry!' But the little mouse was already pelting across the square. 'Mistress Bibo, take our shopping home. I'll be back soon, I hope.' Cardinal Matthias hurried after Cranberry, leaving his cook frightened to death at what might happen to him.

Reaching the end of Vittles Lane, Cranberry saw a tall ship looming out of the smoke-clouds, its guns pointing straight at him. With a squeal of terror, he turned to run, then flung himself flat as the houses to either side trembled to a deafening broadside.

'Cranberry! Come away!' But even as Matthias reached him and dragged him to his feet, the houses burst into flame, blazing timber crashing to the ground as the upper floors collapsed. Matthias flung up his paw to protect his face, and dragged Cranberry back up the street. But another ship, sailing closely behind the first, fired its broadside, roundshot screamed overhead and a house further up the lane collapsed with a roar as loud as the guns, trapping the two mice between searing walls of flame.

Aboard the *Night Crow*, Malatesta watched the destruction he was causing with joy in his evil heart. But now it was time for the next stage of the expedition. The boat carrying the Dirty Tricks squad was already in the water. Gweir, the hooded magician, was with them. Malatesta swung himself over the ship's side and his stoats helped him into the boat.

'Cast off! Row for the western side of the bay, then keep inshore. Once round the point, we head for a fishing village called Abbot's Cove. We must beach the boat away from the village; we don't want to be seen.' His crew rowed strongly; soon, the boat was hidden by the ships. Suddenly, one of the rowers gave a yell of alarm. A ship had rounded the headland and was swooping into the bay. It was the *Avenger*.

6 Tamina to the rescue

Powering between two black-sailed ships, *Avenger*'s guns thundered in a double broadside. Roundshot hammered the enemy hulls and chainshot shrieked through the rigging, shattering spars and bringing masts and sails crashing to the deck. 'Keep going!' yelled Roamer and as Malatesta and his stoats watched in dismay, the ship tore into the harbour. A tower of black sails loomed through the smoke. But even as she fired, *Avenger*'s guns roared and the buccaneers cheered as the enemy ship reeled, splinters flying from her upper deck, gaping holes opening in her side.

'Can't you work some magic?' snarled Malatesta. Gweir gave the ghost of a smile. 'Do you imagine that my powers can be turned on and off to suit you? What I must do later tonight will exhaust me. I cannot waste energy on a ship that you seem unable to cope with!'

With an angry curse, Malatesta gave the order to row away. The last he saw of the *Avenger*, she was vanishing into the smoke-filled harbour.

Through smarting eyes, Roamer peered anxiously ahead. *Avenger* was sailing perilously close to a line of wrecked ships, moored to the quayside; beyond, two mice stood frozen in terror as the houses blazed around them.

'Lord of Light!' yelled Roamer. 'That's the Cardinal and young Cranberry from the 'King's Head'! Bring the ship round! I'm going to help him!'

But someone else had seen the cardinal's peril. Grabbing a line dangling from the mainmast, Princess Tamina swung herself across the narrow strip of water and crashed against the rigging of one of the ruined ships. With a flying leap, she landed on the deck. Pausing to soak her cloak in the water, she vaulted onto the dockside.

'This way!' Tamina threw her soaking cloak over

the two mice and dragged them up a side-alley between blazing houses. Sparks showered down, burning timbers crashed, but Tamina ran on until at last they were clear of the fire.

'That crazy tamarin!' yelled Roamer.

'She's got guts,' grinned Lukas. *'Look out!'*

An enemy ship was looming out of the smoke, all guns blazing. As the shots crashed home, *Avenger* quivered so violently that Cheesemite nearly toppled from the crosstrees. The enemy ship was sweeping alongside, her gun-muzzles almost touching the *Avenger*'s and Roamer yelled: 'Port-guns *fire!'*

Avenger's mighty broadside crashed out. A great shudder passed through the enemy ship as guns were up-ended, spars tumbled to the deck and tongues of flame licked from her stern windows.

'She's a-blaze!' yelled Cheesemite. The wind was pushing the stricken ship away from the dockside. 'Drop anchor!' snapped Roamer. 'Quickly, before –'

A searing spurt of flame shot from the enemy ship, followed by such a thunderous roar that the sea-mice flinched from its awesome power. When its echoes had died away, there were no more enemy ships in sight. The battle was over.

Roamer looked at the crew; their faces, like his,

were black with smoke, their eyes wide and staring. Rio, the burly carpenter, was calmly bandaging the wounded, talking to them cheerfully.

'Well done, lads!' called Roamer. 'Now, where's the princess?'

Tamina, her golden fur singed and blackened, was returning to the quayside with Matthias and Cranberry. As she emerged onto the shattered waterfront, she rapidly scanned the harbour. Of the ship that had blown up, only a few floating spars remained. Beyond, the bay was clear of the enemy.

'Thank you, my dear,' said Matthias.

Tamina grinned. 'That's all right. But Captain Roamer's coming ashore, and I'm afraid he's going to be cross with me.'

Roamer was furious! But as Tamina had saved two lives, there seemed no point in making a scene. 'That was a mad but very brave thing to do, Princess. Are you hurt, Eminence?'

'Not at all, my dear Roamer,' replied the cardinal with a smile. He and the buccaneer were old friends. 'Cranberry and I owe our lives to this brave young tamarin.'

'How did you know I was a tamarin?'

'I wasn't always a cardinal. Once, when I was a young and adventurous mouse, I sailed the

Southern Ocean, and visited your islands. It's many a long year since I last saw one of your tribe. But since you are a princess, your father must be Chief Tia-roa. I remember him well, though he was a young scamp when I knew him! Ah, here comes Cob, Cranberry's father.'

Cranberry, who had been gazing in awe at Tamina, looked round nervously as a stout mouse came puffing to the dockside. 'Cranberry! You crazy kid! Always running into danger! Maybe now you've learned your lesson.' Suddenly, his anger vanished, tears poured down his cheeks and he seized his little son in a hug that left Cranberry gasping for breath. 'But praise to the Lord of Light that you're safe – and you, too, your Eminence.'

'Praise to him indeed,' said Matthias. 'But also to Princess Tamina.'

Cob pulled off his cap and made a clumsy bow. Tamina gave him a dazzling smile, then suddenly remembered that she was supposed to be in charge of the wounded. 'How many hurt?' she asked anxiously.

'Several,' replied Roamer, 'though none fatally. But plenty of nasty cuts from flying splinters and some broken limbs.'

'Bring them ashore, Captain Roamer!' cried Cob.

'We'll take them to the 'King's Head' and look after them there. For them and for all of you, it's drinks on the house, aye, and supper, too!'

'Thanks, Cob,' said Roamer. 'We'll bring them now. The rest must help these mice . . .' Along the waterfront, mice were staring in dismay at their shattered homes, unable to understand what had happened, or why.

From a small, sheltered beach, near the village of Abbot's Cove, Malatesta was counting the black-sailed ships as they sailed out of Aramon bay. 'Only nine! And two of those were leaking like sieves! Who is that accursed mouse who seems intent on wrecking our plans?'

'Name's Roamer,' said a thin-faced stoat called Scratchfur. 'I used to sail in the empress's fleet an' I reco'nise the ship. *Avenger*, twenty-four guns. Very nice – better than some of ours.'

'Shut it!' snapped Malatesta. 'And get up the beach out of sight, all of you. Get some sleep. Scratchfur, since you're so familiar with the *Avenger*, you can take first watch and wake me if you see it. We leave for Aramon at midnight.'

7 The Red Duke

No sooner had the injured buccaneers been ferried ashore, than several earnest-looking mice, wearing spectacles and carrying black bags, appeared at the 'King's Head' and were soon splinting limbs and bandaging busily, helped by Tamina and the cardinal.

Suddenly, the door was flung open to admit a fat, pompous-looking mouse in a magnificent scarlet uniform. A rapier gleamed at his side and two ornate pistols were stuck in his belt. 'Captain Roamer? My name is Balbi, *Captain* Balbi. I don't believe we've met, though of course, like all Aramon, I have heard of your mighty deeds, and it may be that you have heard of me! I have the honour to command Duke Flambeau's bodyguard of Red Lancers.'

Tamina glanced up from her bandaging. 'Who's Duke Flambeau?'

Balbi stared haughtily at the bedraggled, smoke-blackened tamarin. 'I'm astonished you don't know! Duke Flambeau, whom I have the honour to serve, is young King Caladon's uncle. He rules Carminel until the king is old enough.'

'I'd like to meet him.'

Balbi looked Tamina up and down with an insolent stare. 'I was sent to summon Captain Roamer, not the more *common* members of his crew.'

'This is Princess Tamina, daughter of Chief Tia-roa of Coriander and the Golden Islands,' said Roamer quietly.

Balbi gasped in dismay. 'Oh! My dear Princess! Pray forgive me!' he exclaimed, sweeping off his plumed hat in a low bow. 'I am certain the duke would be *delighted* to meet you.'

Tamina curled her lip. 'So kind of you, Captain,' she purred. 'But as you have already observed, I'm not dressed for visiting dukes.' Turning her back on the deeply embarrassed Balbi, Tamina returned to bandaging an injured sea-mouse.

'You certainly put him in his place,' smiled Cardinal Matthias. 'But watch out for him, my dear, he never forgets or forgives!'

Captain Balbi, still smarting from Tamina's snub, led Roamer to the Great Fortress where he left him with a cold bow. The buccaneer made his way to the great hall, which was thronged with mice who had lost their homes in the raid and were hoping for the duke's help. At the far end of the hall, dressed as usual in black velvet and a scarlet cloak, was Flambeau himself. He was seated at a desk, two Red Lancers standing behind him. On the floor was a wooden chest from which Roamer caught the glint of gold.

'Our little tavern were smashed to bits, if it please yer Grace,' a skinny-looking mouse was saying.

'It does not please me!' exclaimed the duke. Plunging his paws into the chest, he scooped up a heap of coins. 'Take twenty gold pieces. It's not much. But it should help pay for the rebuilding.'

Twenty gold pieces was a fortune! As the flabbergasted mice stammered their thanks, others shuffled forward, faces eager, hopes high. 'That duke is the best and kindest of mice,' said the tavern keeper as they left the Hall, clutching their unexpected bounty. It would pay for rebuilding and restocking, with plenty left over!

'Nay, he's a saint!' exclaimed his wife. 'What should we do without him? O'course, he's always been generous; but twenty gold pieces!'

'I wonder what little King Caladon will be like when he's old enough to rule? Not as generous as his uncle, I dare swear!'

So, thought Roamer, the Red Duke's making himself more popular than the king . . .

Duke Flambeau was known as the Red Duke because of his scarlet cloak, and the reddish tinge in his handsome black fur, which marked him as one of the Royal House. Catching sight of Roamer, he spoke loudly to his Guards. 'Give these poor mice everything they need!' The grateful crowd raised a cheer. *'Within reason,'* Flambeau added quietly.

The duke led Roamer into a small, comfortably furnished room. 'You did well today, Captain! Indeed,' he continued, pouring wine for Roamer and himself, 'without you, Aramon might have been destroyed.'

'I doubt that, your Grace,' said Roamer. He had been wondering what Malatesta was up to. The Ermine Lord could have defeated the *Avenger* if he had really tried and the stoats and sea-rats could have taken the city with ease.

A door was suddenly flung open and a sturdy young mouse, his eyes sparkling with pleasure, dashed into the room. 'Roamer!'

'Your Majesty!' exclaimed the duke severely.

King Caladon stopped, his happy welcome crushed. 'Captain Roamer,' he said in a formal voice. 'Welcome home. Thank you for saving Aramon.'

Old Matthias had told Roamer how harshly the Red Duke was treating his nephew; Roamer had not believed him. Now he did; but he kept his thoughts to himself and bowed to the king. 'I am glad to see you again, your Majesty. I have something for you aboard my ship,' he added, with a wink.

'Oh, what is it? When will you bring it?' cried Caladon, his eyes alight once more.

'Your Majesty must withdraw now,' said Duke Flambeau. 'Captain Roamer and I have matters of importance to discuss.'

Caladon had been so looking forward to seeing the famous buccaneer again that for a moment rebellion flared in his heart. But one glance at his uncle's stern face showed him that argument was hopeless. 'Goodbye, Roamer. I have to go now.' He sighed, and trailed miserably out of the room.

Roamer stared after him in dismay. But there was worse to come, for the duke went on: 'Roamer; you and I have never been friends. I have always disapproved of your piracy. I want peace with the Empress Ravanola, but every ship of hers you rob brings us closer to war.'

'That's never stopped you from taking your share of the plunder when we've captured one of her ships,' remarked Roamer.

This was true, but the duke ignored it. 'I am grateful for what you have done today. But thanks to your reckless buccaneering, Empress Ravanola has now made war on Aramon. Fortunately for us, it will soon be time for the winter gales, so no more fleets can threaten us before the Spring. But when the better weather comes . . .'

Mastering his anger, Roamer said: 'Your Grace, Empress Ravanola hungers for power. She would have attacked Carminel sooner or later. But I am convinced that Malatesta's attack today was no more than a diversion.'

'What are you saying?' demanded the duke. 'What do you imagine the Ermine Lord is going to do?'

'I don't know. But he's up to something.'

Flambeau sighed. 'This was obviously a raid to test our defences. You're imagining things.'

'Oh, no I'm not. Nor am I imagining the way you're treating King Caladon. He looks miserable. Isn't he allowed any fun?'

'Fun? Caladon must learn how to be king. There's no time for *fun*.'

Roamer's temper boiled over. 'By the time he's old enough for kingship, you'll have taken all his power – yes, and crushed the spirit out of him!'

The Red Duke's whiskers quivered with rage. 'How dare you! I could have you flung in the dungeons for that!'

Roamer narrowed his eyes. 'Are you threatening me, Flambeau?'

The duke hesitated. Roamer was popular in Aramon. He must not anger him. At least, not yet . . . Flambeau smiled. 'My apologies, Captain,' he said smoothly. 'I bear a heavy responsibility and this raid has upset me more than you realise. Perhaps you're right about Caladon. Perhaps he should have some – er – fun. But that's my business, not yours. You may go.'

Lukas was waiting for Roamer on the quayside. The big sea-mouse was full of questions; but after one look at his captain's face, he decided to keep them to himself! Roamer was angry at Flambeau's insults, and seething over his treatment of Caladon.

He was also puzzling about Malatesta's raid. What on earth was that wily stoat up to?

The eleven chimes from the Great Cathedral sounded faintly on the beach near Abbot's Cove. Malatesta gave the sleeping Gweir a shake. 'Wake up, wizard! It's time.'

Gweir rose stiffly to his feet and took up his staff. 'I am ready. At midnight, I shall raise such a tempest that no mouse will wish to venture out-of-doors. You may carry out your task in perfect safety.'

Once again, Malatesta wished that he could do without the wizard's help. Gweir always made him feel uneasy, such was the power that radiated from him.

'You are wishing that I was back in Ravanola's palace?' sneered Gweir.

Malatesta silently cursed himself. The wizard could read his mind like an open book. Gweir laughed. 'I care nothing for your wishes! All I care about is the glorious destiny that awaits our empress!'

The wizard strode away into the darkness. Malatesta scowled after him. Gradually dislike of Gweir faded as he thought about the adventure that lay ahead. At midnight, he shook his stoats awake. 'Come on! It's time to help ourselves to that ruby!'

8 Princess in peril

'Some more mangoes and cream, Princess?' asked Mother Bibo.

'Oh, I couldn't!' Princess Tamina leaned back in her seat, feeling as if her tummy would burst. She grinned round the candlelit table at the cardinal and the dozen or so orphans who had shared the banquet. Matthias, as usual, had eaten sparingly but the little mice were leaning back in their seats, tummies bulging out of their rags after mountains of salmon and a double helping of mangoes and cream.

'I expect you're looking forward to the birthday,'

said Tamina to the young mouse seated beside her. His name was Spital.

'You mean the Lord o' Light's birthday?' Spital shrugged and licked the mango juice from his paws. 'S'pose so. All them lights in the sky.'

Once a year, in the depths of winter, the sky erupted in a magical blaze of colour and light. It always happened on the night of the Lord of Light's birthday and reminded the mice that their god still lived and was watching over them. But Tamina had not been thinking of the midnight lights.

'I mean *presents*! What do you want this year?' Tamina's father had promised her a sailboat. The previous year, he had given her a necklace of coral and pearl, the year before that a diamond pendant, and the year before that –

Spital looked blank. 'Dunno. Got an apple last year.'

'I got an orange,' said another mouse.

'I didn't get nuffink,' whispered a third. His name was Chowdmouse, and he was the smallest orphan there.

The cardinal murmured in Tamina's ear: 'These children are poor, my dear, and have no parents to care for them. Each year, I try to find money for presents. But it is not easy, for there are so many orphans, more than are with us tonight.'

For the rest of the meal, Tamina was unusually quiet. When it was time for her to return to the ship, Mother Bibo brought her cloak. 'I've brushed and sponged it, dear, but I'm afraid it still smells of burning from when you were rescuing the cardinal and that scamp, Cranberry.'

Tamina flung the cloak round her shoulders and thanked the old cook with a dazzling smile and a kiss. As Matthias opened the door for her, she took out her purse and gave it to him. 'Please take this. Use it to buy presents for the children.'

Tamina had plenty of pocket money. The purse was bulging with gold. But before Matthias could say a word, Tamina had gone.

The cardinal lived in that part of Aramon called the Mankinoles. Many poor mice lived there, as well as artists, poets and university scholars. Even at this late hour, the streets were crowded, and filled with delicious smells from the cheap taverns and cook-shops. In the small square, where Casey and the beavers were eating their picnic supper, coloured lanterns twinkled in the trees. As Tamina strolled through the cheerful crowds, several mice nudged one another and pointed her out as the tamarin princess who had rescued their cardinal. Normally, this would have filled her with pride. But tonight she was feeling something she had never felt before: the pleasure of having done something for others less fortunate than herself.

As midnight approached, Gweir toiled to the summit of the hill overlooking the city. For a while, he rested, preparing himself. Then, raising his staff above his head, he invoked the dreadful power of Viperius, the Snake-god, whom the stoats believed dwelt in a cave far beneath Ravanola's palace in Kalamaris: the House of the Snake.

> *Mighty Snake-god, send the lightning!*
> *From the sky let torrents fall!*
> *Let the storm clouds burst asunder,*
> *Let the sky be rent with thunder!*
> *Viperius, I call upon you,*
> *Snake-god, mightiest of all!*

A cold wind blasted the hilltop. Rolling clouds smothered the stars. Suddenly, a dazzling flash of lightning lit up the city, a roar of thunder shook the ground and Gweir raised his hood as a thick curtain of rain sluiced down. Within seconds, every mouse in Aramon would be scuttling for shelter.

As it was peacetime, the gates were never closed. Mice patrolled the walls; but they were running from the storm to the shelter of their guardhouses. Malatesta's squad could enter the city in perfect safety. Wearily, for much power had flowed through him, Gweir trudged down the hill, heading for Abbot's Cove, where the stoat lord would shortly be waiting.

When the storm struck, Tamina had left the Mankinoles and entered the more respectable part of the city, where shops and taverns were closed and the houses were in darkness. Pelting through the downpour, she sought shelter beneath the porch of a house. But rain was flooding through the thatch and she was quickly drenched. This is hopeless, she thought; I must find somewhere else. But the rain had turned the narrow lanes to rivers, the lightning was bouncing all around her and the houses trembled to the thunder's roar. Every step was an effort and she had to make several stops in shop doorways. At last, the Great Cathedral reared above her. Shelter at last, she thought gratefully, as she splashed up the steps and pushed open the door.

Like tall trees in a dark forest, two long lines of pillars stretched to the far end of the cathedral where, at the top of a wide staircase, a solitary candle illuminated the High Altar. As her eyes adjusted to the darkness, Tamina gazed in awe at the great arches, soaring to the invisible roof. Suddenly, her fur began to tingle, a strange, alien smell hit her and all her instincts cried out 'Danger!'

She crept to one of the side aisles and peeped from behind a pillar. Not a shadow moved. But Tamina was certain that enemies were somewhere about. Her cloak was heavy with rainwater; it would hinder her if she had to run – or fight. She slipped it off and laid it on the floor. Then, she inched forward until she reached the next pillar. Now she could see, beneath the candle, a high glass dome. Beneath it, on a velvet cushion, lay the softly glowing Ruby of Power.

Though she had never seen it before, Tamina had heard of this, the greatest treasure of Carminel. She moved to the next pillar, pausing for a moment in its shadow. She peered round it, and stifled a gasp. At the foot of the wide staircase, tall iron railings kept all but the priests away from the altar. But the gate in the railings stood open and a shadowy figure was gliding up the steps.

Despite its heavy cloak, Tamina recognised it as a stoat. She had seen some of them during her life on the islands and had learned to fear them. Slowly, the figure lifted the glass dome and set it to one side. At once, an angry light gleamed from the ruby; but in one rapid movement, the stoat tilted the cushion, tipping the ruby into a small sack.

Tamina held her breath. More stoats had emerged from the opposite aisle and were waiting at the iron gate. Tamina crouched on all fours and crept to the next pillar.

Malatesta hid the sack among the folds of his cloak. He could feel the presence of the mouse-god, the Lord of Light, in this house of shadows; now that he had the ruby, he could hardly wait to get outside. He called softly: 'Piebald! Scratchfur! We're leaving!' From the far side of the nave, two other stoats appeared. Tamina froze. She gave a cautious sniff. But there was no trace of an enemy on her side of the nave.

A sudden flash of lightning lit up the cathedral. Malatesta's white cloak glimmered like a ghost. The raiders had reached the end of the nave and were almost at the door when Scratchfur said: 'Wait a bit! I smell somethin' funny!'

'So what?' snapped Malatesta. 'Let's get out of here.'

'No, wait. It's a sort of burnt smell. Comin' from over there.'

He hurried across to the side aisle and searched among the shadows. Malatesta stood fuming by the door. 'Whatever it is, leave it!'

'Found it! Only an old cloak. Soakin' wet. Don't arf pong.'

Malatesta's paw was on the latch. 'All right, let's go . . . What did you say?'

'I said it pongs.'

Malatesta strode over to where Scratchfur was holding the cloak. 'Soaking wet,' he murmured. 'Someone's just come in. The cloak smells of burning, but I can smell something else . . . *tamarin*!'

Tamina did not wait to be caught. Leaping to her feet, she sprinted along a row of chairs to the centre aisle and fled towards the altar, hearing the stoats pounding after her. There must be another way out, she thought – and there it was, a little, low door, over to her right. She ran towards it, but Scratchfur was pounding up the side aisle and he flung himself in front of the door. Tamina took a flying leap and her booted feet caught Scratchfur straight in the stomach. As he collapsed with a grunt of agony, Tamina recovered her balance, jumped over him and twisted the door handle. But the door was locked and Tamina spun round, snarling, as the stoats closed in.

9 Caladon defiant

Early next morning, Roamer descended deep into the *Avenger*'s hold, following the sound of hammering and the powerful stench of tar. 'How's it going, Rio?'

'I nearly finish, Capitano.' The carpenter paused from his hammering and mopped his brow. 'A nail here, a nail there, a coat of tar and the *Avenger*, she ready for anything!'

'Good. Let me know when you've finished. Have you seen the princess this morning?'

Rio grinned. 'That crazy tamarin? No. I reckon she got up early, went to the 'King's Head' tavern to see to the wounded. Then I guess she go shoppin' – she got plenty gold!'

As Roamer emerged on deck, Cranberry, Spital and Chowdmouse came pelting, wild-eyed, up the gangplank. 'Captain Roamer!' yelled Cranberry. 'Message from the cardinal! He's found Princess Tamina's cloak in the Great Cathedral and she ain't nowhere to be seen. He says will you come at once!'

Yelling for Lukas to follow him, Roamer ran down the gangplank and set off up Vittles Lane. After the storm, the sky was blue and sunlight sparkled on the puddles. The lane was already thronged with early shoppers and loud with the merchants' cries of 'What do ye lack? Come buy, come buy! Fresh oranges, lovely red apples, dates an' figs for the Lord o' Light's birthday!' But Roamer ignored the cheerful scene. After yesterday's raid, he was convinced that Malatesta had been up to something; now he feared that the stoats had indeed come ashore and that Tamina had found them.

Matthias was waiting for them in the cathedral. He was holding Tamina's cloak. 'She must have sought shelter from the storm,' said the cardinal. 'But I fear something has happened to her. Come with me.'

Roamer and Lukas followed him down the side aisle. 'This door is kept locked. But look . . .'

Several chairs were upturned and the dust on the floor showed a mass of paw-marks. 'Looks like there's been a struggle,' said Roamer. 'Hello, what's this?' Delving under a chair, he picked up a brass button. It was engraved with a spider.

'Ravanola's sign! I should have guessed. There were stoats in here last night, and they must have found Tamina. There was a struggle, and she –'

'Got caught,' finished Lukas, scowling at the scuff-marks. 'But what were the stoats doin' here?'

'There's only one thing they'd have been after,' said the cardinal; 'the ruby. But it's still here.'

The buccaneers looked towards the High Altar. Beneath its glass dome, the jewel was winking in the sunlight. 'I must go,' said Matthias. 'I shall tell the Red Duke what has happened. Then, I must return to the Mankinholes; the poor and the sick are waiting for me. Last night, Tamina gave me enough gold to buy a home for my orphans. I cannot bear to think of her in danger. You'll find her, won't you?'

'If I have to sail to the ends of the earth,' said Roamer grimly. 'And when I've found her, heaven help Malatesta!'

As the cardinal hurried away, Roamer said: 'There's nothing more to be done here. Let's get back to the ship. As soon as Rio's finished, we'll set sail and find Tamina if it's the last thing we do.'

The buccaneers were almost at the door when Cranberry came pelting down the aisle. 'Captain, wait! Spital's found something.'

Spital was crouching by the iron gates leading to the High Altar. 'Someone's tried to pick this 'ere lock.'

Roamer and Lukas bent to examine the scratches surrounding the keyhole. 'But they failed,' said Lukas. 'The ruby's still there.'

'I wonder,' said Roamer thoughtfully. 'Lukas, do you think you could open this gate?'

'Easy!' Lukas placed the point of his dagger inside the huge lock. He moved it up and down, then left and right until they heard a loud click and the door swung open. Roamer led the way up the steps. Lifting the glass dome, he placed it to one side. For a long time, he stared at the ruby. Then, he reached out his paw and picked it up.

'Captain Roamer! What do you think you're doing?' Duke Flambeau and Captain Balbi were running up the steps. Cranberry, Spital and Chowdmouse immediately dodged behind Lukas's broad back. They were afraid of the Red Duke.

'I was just going to ask Lukas what he thought about the Great Ruby of Carminel.'

'It's very fine, Skipper,' said Lukas with a grin.

'But we've lifted better ones from the sea-rats!'

'Blasphemy!' cried Balbi, hopping up and down, his eyes bulging. 'You ignorant clodhopper! Why, that ruby –'

'Is *not* the Ruby of Power,' snapped Roamer. 'The real ruby has a tiny beating heart. This one doesn't. What's more, the ruby exists to protect the Royal House, and always glows when a member of it is near. You, your Grace, are the king's uncle. But this ruby isn't glowing.'

'You mean – it's a fake?' gasped Balbi.

'No, it's real. But it's not the Ruby of Power. Malatesta's taken that, so that when Ravanola invades, we shall be deprived of its protection.'

'Clever of him,' murmured Flambeau. 'No one ever comes this close to the ruby, except the priests and they'd only see what they were expecting to see. Captain Roamer, you must set sail at once! Rescue the ruby!'

'And our princess,' whispered Chowdmouse.

The news that Malatesta had taken Tamina ran like a shockwave through the *Avenger*. When the news reached the 'King's Head', the wounded buccaneers hobbled back to the ship, furious that their princess had been captured and desperate to sail to the rescue. By midday, Rio and his carpenters had completed their repairs, and the rest of the crew, sent out by Roamer to scour the markets for food, water and beer, returned with enough provisions to last a year. By the time the ammunition lockers had been replenished with new cannonballs and the powder magazine restocked with fresh barrels of gunpowder, the sun was sinking, the sea-mice were ready and the *Avenger* was tugging at her anchor on the ebbing tide, as if impatient to set sail.

Suddenly, Roamer remembered something. 'Caladon's present! I must take it, Lukas. I promised him. I shan't be long.'

At the Great Fortress, the Red Duke was in his study, working on an important-looking document. As Roamer entered, Flambeau looked up in surprise and let his sleeve fall, as if by accident, over the document. 'Why haven't you sailed?' he demanded angrily.

'I forgot this.' From under his cloak, Roamer took out a beautiful model of the *Avenger*, complete with sails and rigging. He had made it himself. 'It's for Caladon.'

'Oh, very well,' said Flambeau, impatiently. 'I'll take it to him. Now go!'

Outside the door, Roamer paused. He was wondering why Flambeau had been so careful not to let him see that document. The duke had looked furtive, almost guilty . . . Following those instincts that rarely let him down, Roamer slipped behind one of the fine tapestries that lined the Great Hall and waited. At last, Flambeau came out. Roamer counted to ten, and followed.

He padded silently behind the duke along dimly-lit passages and up spiral staircases cloaked in shadow. At last, Flambeau reached a long, tapestry-hung corridor. He entered a room, shutting the door behind him. Roamer crept to the door and listened.

'I won't sign.'

'Oh, but you will.' Flambeau's silky voice was full of menace. But Caladon refused to be intimidated.

'I can't! If I do, you take all my power as king!'

'Foolish child! With the ruby missing, we face great danger. For the good of the country, I must take full royal power. Now sign!'

'There's no danger,' said Caladon stubbornly. 'Roamer will get the ruby back.'

The mention of Roamer reminded Flambeau. 'The captain sends you this.'

'Oh! It's the *Avenger*! Roamer – or Lukas – must have made it! It's beautiful!'

'If you do not sign, I will smash it.'

After a long silence, Caladon said quietly: 'Don't

smash it. I won't sign. But please don't smash the ship. Give it to some other child . . . No!'

Outside the door, Roamer flinched at the crash and the splintering of wood as Flambeau hurled the ship to the floor and stamped on it. 'That's nothing to what I will do! You will be deprived of food and drink until you obey me. I shall put it about that you are ill, and that no one is to go near you. I shall come back tomorrow morning. Around breakfast time. Except you won't be having any. Then perhaps you'll sign, you stubborn, defiant little fool!'

10 Escape

Footsteps approached the door. Roamer darted behind a tapestry and pressed himself against the wall, listening for the slam and the click as Flambeau turned the key. Peeping out, Roamer watched as the duke hurried down the corridor, his long shadow trailing behind.

Remembering how Lukas had picked the lock in the cathedral, Roamer gave Caladon's door the same treatment. As he flung it open, Caladon's joy at seeing him turned to excitement when Roamer said: 'You're coming with me. I won't leave you here for that brute to torment.'

'Am I sailing with you?' He stared sorrowfully at the wreckage on the floor. 'I wouldn't sign his stupid paper, so he smashed the ship. I'm sorry.'

'Don't be. You did well. But I daren't take you aboard the *Avenger*, it's too dangerous, though I'll make sure Flambeau thinks I have. I'll take you to the cardinal's house in the Mankinoles. He'll look after you, so on with your boots and your cloak, and we'll be off. Is there another way out of here?'

Drawing aside one of the curtains that lined the walls, Caladon revealed a low door. 'My private staircase! Only to be used in time of danger. That's now, I reckon. It leads to the postern gate at the rear of the fortress.'

'That'll be guarded. But it can't be helped. Let's go.'

The dark, narrow staircase smelt musty with disuse. For what felt like an eternity, they crept down, feeling their way over the uneven treads. At last, a glimmer of light appeared, the steps ended and a passage stretched to a low door.

'The postern gate,' whispered Roamer. 'I'll go first.'

Gently, he eased back the bolts. As he opened the door, the Red Lancer standing guard outside spun round with a cry of alarm. 'Who's that? Why, Captain Roamer! What on earth are you –'

Roamer slammed his fist into the sentry's jaw and

the mouse slumped to the ground. Using the guard's own braces, Roamer swiftly tied his paws and ankles, and gagged him with the mouse's own scarf. 'They'll soon find him. We must hurry!'

Roamer hurried Caladon through the dark streets until they reached the bright lights of the Mankinoles. Plunging into the old clothes' market, Roamer bought Caladon an ancient woollen cap, pulling it down so that it concealed the little mouse's distinctive reddish-black fur. Hoping that no one would notice Caladon's rich cloak, Roamer led him through the noisy streets towards the cardinal's house.

But as they crossed the square, they saw Matthias hurrying towards them with Cranberry, Spital and Chowdmouse. 'Roamer!' cried the cardinal. 'I've heard about the ruby. What a dreadful thing! We were coming to the harbour to see you off. But what are you doing here?'

'Looking for you, Eminence.' Roamer lowered his voice and in a few words explained what had happened. 'I dare not take Caladon with me. Can you hide him?'

Cranberry and his friends were gazing in awe at the young king. 'Us'll hide him,' said Chowdmouse huskily.

But Matthias shook his head. 'Flambeau will turn

the city upside down to find him. He would be safer away from Aramon.'

'But where?' asked Roamer. 'And who would take him?'

Caladon had never been in the Mankinoles. He was staring open-mouthed, revelling in the strange sights and enticing new smells. Catching sight of Casey and his friends, he said: 'Who are they?'

'Them's the beavers,' said Spital. 'Packin' up to go 'ome. They got a schooner up by the water gate, on the Aramon River. When the tide turns –'

'Captain Roamer!' exclaimed Cranberry. 'Caladon could go with the beavers!'

'Yeah,' whispered Chowdmouse, wishing he had thought of it first.

The beavers were just heaving on their backpacks. Another minute and they would have gone. Roamer and Matthias hurried over to them.

'Why, it's the cardinal!' cried Casey. 'Come to say goodbye? Say, is that Cap'n Roamer with you? Hey, fellas, come an' meet the cap'n!'

As the beavers crowded round, Roamer said: 'The cardinal and I have a favour to ask. King Caladon is in danger. Will you take him to the mountains, and the protection of Lord Marengo and the eagles?'

'Trouble with the Red Duke, huh?' muttered

Casey. 'Well, I ain't surprised. Sure we'll take him! Where is he?'

'I'm here.' Caladon pulled off his cap, and the lantern-light fell on his reddish-black fur. Casey grinned a welcome. 'Mighty proud to meet you, young sir. Say, you ever bin aboard a schooner? No? Well, I guess there ain't no time like the present!'

Aboard the *Avenger*, Lukas was anxiously scanning the dockside. He was just about to send out a search party, when Roamer came running up the gangplank and ordered it pulled in after him. But scarcely had he joined Lukas on the quarterdeck than a dozen Red Lancers, led by Captain Balbi, swarmed on to the quayside. The sentry at the postern gate had been discovered and the furious Flambeau had wasted no time in ordering a search for the king, starting with the *Avenger*.

Balbi had not forgotten how Roamer had made a fool of him in front of Princess Tamina. Puffing himself up until his stomach threatened to burst his tunic, he bawled: 'Captain Roamer! This ship is under arrest, by order of Duke Flambeau! You must release King Caladon at once, and give yourself up!'

'What's he on about?' asked Lukas.

'No time to explain,' muttered Roamer. 'But Balbi thinks the king's aboard, and we must make him believe it. His Majesty is asleep in his cabin,' he shouted, 'and under my protection! So get off the dockside!'

This was just what Balbi had been hoping for. 'You will learn that you cannot defy my commands, Roamer!' He grinned round at his soldiers. 'Red Lancers, open fire!'

The sea-mice flung themselves flat as bullets whined through the rigging and thumped into *Avenger*'s side. As the Lancers hastily reloaded, Roamer yelled: 'Starboard guns! Run out!' The soldiers froze in horror as twelve long cannons rumbled into view. 'Gun-crews, stand by!' roared Roamer. With a squeal of terror, Balbi fled, closely followed by his troopers.

'Just as well,' said Lukas, as the red cloaks fluttered away up Vittles Lane. 'Our guns ain't loaded. But what in the world's goin' on?'

'Tell you later,' grinned Roamer. 'Get the ship under way!'

At Lukas's command, sea-mice swarmed up the rigging and out along the dizzy heights of the yard-arms. At the cry of '*Anchor's a-weigh*!' the sails thundered down, Lukas spun the wheel and *Avenger* glided out of the harbour.

Meanwhile, Spital was leading Caladon and the

beavers along deserted back-alleys, Cranberry and Chowdmouse bringing up the rear. Cardinal Matthias had gone home, not wishing to draw attention to the beavers' party by his presence. But they met no one. Reaching the narrow river which flowed through Aramon, they followed it to the water gate on the eastern edge of the city. Moored to the quayside was the beavers' schooner, the *Eaglet*.

'All clear!' called Spital. The beavers hurried aboard and began setting the sails. In a moment, the tide would turn and the powerful current would carry the schooner upriver. Caladon hurried eagerly up the gangplank. Suddenly, he stopped, turned back and held out his paws to his three faithful friends. 'You three risked your lives for me tonight. I shall never forget that.'

'When will you come back, yer Majesty?' asked Cranberry.

Caladon had not thought about that. Now he did. 'By next spring, I shall be fully grown. Well, almost. That's when I'll come back and I'll bring Lord Marengo and the eagles! Together we'll kick out my uncle!'

'We'll be almost grown-up too,' said Spital. 'Can we fight for you?'

'I'll fight,' whispered Chowdmouse.

Caladon grinned. 'There'll be plenty of fighting! Not just against my uncle and his Red Lancers but against Malatesta, too, I shouldn't wonder. I shall need plenty of mice to fight for me and for Carminel. But you three must be my personal bodyguard.'

'Come aboard, sir!' called Casey. 'The tide's turned!'

The beavers cast off the moorings, the breeze filled the sails and the *Eaglet* surged out into midstream. The three mice waved until she slipped beneath the watergate and was swallowed up in the darkness. 'Personal bodyguard!' grinned Cranberry. 'Cor! I can't wait till Spring!'

PART TWO
THE LORD OF SHADOWS

11 Storm

Aboard *Night Crow*, Malatesta was sunning himself in a deck chair, watching the sea-rats trimming the sails to the wind, scrubbing the decks and cleaning the big guns. The Ermine Lord was feeling pleased with himself. His mission had been a brilliant success, and he could look forward to a rich reward from the old Black Widow, to add to his already vast fortune.

Of course, those foolish mice would never spot the imitation ruby; and it would be amusing to see what Ravanola would do with that interfering tamarin, now trussed up in the hold under lock and key. As for Roamer, Malatesta expected him to race to the princess's rescue like the fool he was! That was why the Ermine Lord had taken her with him and as soon as *Avenger* was sighted, Malatesta knew exactly what he was going to do.

In her damp, foul-smelling prison, Tamina had long given up the struggle to free herself. The stoats had tied her up so tightly she was quite unable to reach the little dagger hidden in her left boot. As she lay helpless, wondering what would happen to her in Salamex, she heard Scratchfur's voice calling from the masthead: 'Sir! Strange sail on the eastern horizon!'

Malatesta clapped a telescope to his eye and saw a tall white pyramid. The ship was moving swiftly, and, as Malatesta watched, more sails were spread across the mastheads: top-gallants and royals, to give the ship yet more speed.

'It's the *Avenger*!' yelled Scratchfur. Tamina's heart leapt but the Ermine Lord's next words made her blood run cold. 'Gweir! You're good at raising storms. Sink that accursed pirate!'

Gweir smiled at the thought of Roamer's death. Raising his staff, he once more invoked Pythius, the Snake-god. As he chanted his spell, the eastern horizon grew dark, curving bands of rain and hail poured to the sea, lightning lanced down and the air quivered to peal after peal of thunder. Malatesta laughed; for through his telescope, he could just make out the *Avenger* running helplessly before the storm before the darkness blotted her out.

There had been no time for the buccaneers to take in the sails; the wind had blasted them in seconds, leaving them flying in tatters. 'Get below, all of you!' yelled Roamer. But as his mice scuttled for the hatches, Lukas and Ben, their backs bent to the wind, struggled to the quarterdeck where Roamer was wrestling with the wheel, trying to hold the ship on course.

'Us'll stay with you, zur!' yelled Ben. But even their combined strength could not hold the wheel. 'No use!' shouted Roamer. 'We're being driven south instead of west, but we can't fight this storm! Let her go!' The three mice leaped away and clung for dear life to the stern railings. The wheel spun wildly and the ship heeled over, white water pouring across her bows as she plunged into a deep trough between mountainous waves. With the deck tilting perilously, the mice struggled back to the wheel, striving to hold it, though it twitched and tugged at their paws; but the wind was behind them now, they held the wheel steady at last, and the *Avenger*'s mastheads, which had been dipping almost to the water, slowly rose again.

All day and well into the night, Roamer and his faithful friends held the ship on her southerly course. But by midnight, they were exhausted and Rio, staggering to the quarterdeck, reported that the ship was leaking badly and the crew were labouring at the pumps. Roamer knew they could not go on much longer.

'Look, Captain!' Lukas was yelling above the roaring wind. Directly ahead, white water was foaming above a long, submerged reef. If *Avenger* struck that, they were finished.

The three sea-mice hauled at the wheel but the wind was too strong, and the ship ploughed on. At that moment, Roamer and his companions tasted death on the salty spray that was lashing the deck.

'Zur! Look there!' Directly above, the clouds had parted to reveal a brilliant star. Suddenly, its beams streaked down, turning the *Avenger*'s bows to silver; and, as Roamer stared in wonder, the ship swung away from the reef and they saw, low on the horizon, a distant island.

'That's Coriander!' shouted Lukas.

'And that were the star of the Lord o' Light,' said

Ben. 'Reckon he's saved us.' Roamer felt relief and gratitude flooding through him. He stared back at that black, churning reef. Never had he and his crew been so close to death.

As dawn broke, the battered *Avenger* limped into Coriander Bay. The storm had carried away her topmasts, she was leaking like a sieve, her crew were bruised, battered and exhausted. But they were alive; and their determination to recover the ruby and rescue their princess was as strong as ever.

When the buccaneers had wearily dragged themselves ashore, the tamarins took over the ship. They sailed her round to a narrow creek and let the tide carry her onto the beach. For many days and nights, the air rang to saw and hammer as the tamarins laboured to repair the damage, while the weary crew lay beneath the palm trees, recovering their strength and gorging themselves on grilled fish, sweetcorn, mangoes and melons.

'Where do you suppose Malatesta will have taken Tamina?' asked Roamer. It was his second day on the island. Trying to ignore his bruises and aching limbs, he had climbed to the chief's treehouse and the two of them were squatting on the rush mats, sipping mango juice.

'To the House of the Snake,' came the grim reply.

'The empress's palace. The city of Kalamaris lies on the slopes of a steep hill. The palace stands at the top.'

'Tell me about the city. Everything you know. Draw me a map, if you can. As soon as my ship's ready and my crew have recovered, we sail for Kalamaris. When next you see us, old friend, I pledge my word that we shall have Tamina – and the ruby!'

Before leaving Aramon, Roamer had ordered his crew to scour the dockside stores for black sailcloth and paint. When *Avenger* finally sailed out of Coriander Bay, she had been transformed. Black sails hung from her spars, and Rio's skilful carpentry had disguised her sleek lines so that her fore- and after-decks stood higher than before. Her proud name had been painted out and replaced with 'Scorpion', a name, so Tia-roa assured Roamer, used by several ships in the empress's fleet. A week later, as a full moon climbed the sky, the *Scorpion* was creeping towards the enemy coast.

They could have arrived sooner. But Tia-roa had told Roamer something that had fired the sea-mouse's imagination. Though winter would soon hold Carminel in its icy grip, the Empire of Salamex blazed with summer heat; and upon this night, the lights in the sky that marked the Lord of Light's birthday also appeared over Salamex. There, they were taken as a sign of the Snake-god's power and the city celebrated with a riotous Carnival of Masks. The mean, twisting streets were bright with coloured lanterns and the stoats and sea-rats, all wearing masks, danced and drank the night away.

Among the treasures stowed in the *Avenger*'s hold were several bolts of multicoloured silk. Ever since leaving Coriander, the sailmakers had been busy, stitching gaudy costumes. As the ship glided into the harbour and dropped anchor, the mice saw that the city was ablaze with coloured lights, and music and laughter sounded clearly across the still water. Roamer ordered the cutter to be launched and called the twenty sea-mice of the landing-party to the ship's side.

Each mouse was dressed in silken shirt and trousers, their brilliant colours merging and rippling in the lantern-light. To complete the disguise, every mouse wore a snake's head carnival mask, made of dyed sail-cloth, with jewels for eyes and small slits to see through. Each mask had a red strip stitched across the top so that the mice could recognise each other.

'You all know what to do,' said Roamer. 'But remember: Tia-roa told me that though the palace gardens are open tonight, the ways into the palace itself, the House of the Snake, are guarded.'

'By the Ermine Guard, Captain?' asked Cheesemite. 'We can deal with them!'

'No. They are guarded by the empress's spiders.'

'That's all right! Who's afraid of them?' Cheesemite's voice sounded bold, but his eyes had lost some of their sparkle. Most of the landing-party looked subdued. No one liked the idea of taking on the spiders.

'You *should* be afraid of them!' said Roamer. 'They're as venomous and deadly as their mistress, so be very careful. But the Lord of Light saved us from drowning, and his star will be watching over us tonight. Have you all got pistols and knives?' Twenty snake-heads nodded. 'Wish us luck, Lukas. If we're not back by dawn, raise the anchor and sail home.'

'If you ain't back by dawn, I'll give this devil's city a couple of broadsides, then lead the rest of the lads ashore! We'll find you, wherever you are!'

Roamer laughed. 'Let's hope it doesn't come to that! Now, is the cutter ready? Then let's go!'

12 The blind spot

'Ermine Guards to starb'd, zur!' Even on land, old Ben liked to use sea language. As he and Roamer climbed the steep main street of Kalamaris, they were uncomfortably aware of several Ermine Guards prowling through the noisy carnival crowds.

Getting ashore had been easy. Several parties of masked sea-rats were rowing in from ships in the harbour, so nobody paid any attention to the *Avenger*'s cutter. It seemed that the whole city was dancing, some in couples, several in long chains, dipping and swaying through narrow, lantern-lit streets. Most dancers were masked, like the sea-mice, with silken snake-heads, though some of the richer stoats were showing off with vulture masks festooned with real feathers. But as Roamer and Ben slipped through the crowds, and began to climb towards the palace, they spotted several more Ermine Guards. They were not masked, or joining in the fun, but still, silent, and watchful.

Meanwhile, the crew were taking up their positions. On street corners or outside noisy taverns and bars, the sea-mice joined in the dancing and laughter. But they were careful not to stray too far from their agreed places, knowing that Roamer and Ben would need them later to cover their retreat to the cutter with Princess Tamina and the ruby.

In the palace garden, a band of sea-rats was playing loud music; masked revellers were dancing, or sauntering across the lawn and down the shadowy grassy paths. As Roamer and Ben wandered casually through the unguarded gates, they noticed that every entrance to the palace was barred by a spider of Ravanola's bodyguard. Of the empress herself, there was no sign.

'Them spiders are unarmed,' whispered Ben.

'You think so? Each has enough poison to kill our entire crew.'

Ben and Roamer ambled round the garden, talking and laughing while studying the palace defences. Around its edges, the building was only a single storey high, but its white walls rose sheer, with never a foothold. At last, they came to the rear of the building. Nobody else was about. Light flooded through an open archway, but the spider-guard's shadow lay long across the grass.

As they turned another corner, Roamer stopped abruptly and dragged Ben into the shadow of the wall. 'I've found it! The blind spot! Every wall has an arch, every arch has a spider, and every corner is a sharp angle *except this one*! It's curved – probably because the garden slopes away so steeply here, down that bare slope to the trees, and the wall follows the curve of the ground. Where we are now, the spiders can't see us! And another thing; every corner has one of those stone gargoyles sticking out from the top of the wall. They're all in the shape of a spider, did you notice? This curve has one as well. Get your rope ready, Ben. We're going up!'

Ben unwound the rope hidden beneath his tunic. On the first throw, the loop caught round the spider-gargoyle. Ben pulled the noose tight and Roamer climbed. As he hooked his legs round the gargoyle, and hoisted himself onto the flat roof, Ben followed, drawing the rope up after him.

Quickly, they ducked out of sight behind the parapet. The roof stretched before them, rising in a series of wide ridges. From the top came a distant glow. 'Skylight,' whispered Roamer. 'Come on.'

They scuttled across the roof on all fours. As they climbed over the ridges, they could see the twinkling lights of the harbour and the dark sea beyond. Somewhere out there, the *Avenger* was waiting.

Roamer inched forward until he could peer down through the glass of the skylight. One glance was enough. 'Take a look, Ben.'

Ben poked his snout over the edge. 'Oh, Lord o'Light,' he murmured.

Far below, lay the empress's throne-room. From silken rings high on one wall, the slender golden strands of Ravanola's great web stretched diagonally almost to the middle of the room. In front of it, a mosaic path encircled the pit where the coils of the Salamex viper, the god-on-earth, gleamed in the lamplight. Against the opposite wall, a huge snake reared its head. It was made of painted stone, but was so lifelike that in the lamplight its scales seemed to move. Within its gaping jaws, dull and lifeless, lay the Ruby of Carminel.

* * *

The 'Green Toad' was a small tavern halfway between the harbour and the palace. It was crowded with stoats and sea-rats, all managing to pour ale down their throats in spite of their masks. At a table by the open window sat Rio and Cheesemite.

'How much longer, Rio?'

The big carpenter shrugged. 'Who knows? Any time now, the capitano, he come a-runnin' down the street wi' da ruby an' our princess, an' maybe there's some shootin'. Don't be scared, Cheesemite. Rio take care of you –'

'Join us in a drink, friends!' Two foaming mugs of ale appeared on the table. The mice glanced up in alarm. Two stoats wearing snake-masks loomed above them and a loud, cheery voice said: 'Judgin' by your tails, you two must be sea-rats! What ship?'

Cheesemite gulped; but Rio answered confidently: 'The *Scorpion*! And we'll take a wet with pleasure!' Cheesemite was astonished; Rio's accent had vanished and he sounded exactly like one of the enemy.

'Scratchfur's the name,' said the stoat. 'An' this is my mate, Piebald. We're Ermine Guard, Dirty Tricks squad, just back from a raid on Aramon!'

Rio's cackle of laughter was bloodcurdling. 'You got plenty of plunder, friend, I'll be bound!'

Scratchfur spat in disgust through the open window. 'Not a penny! We was on a secret mission with old Testy 'imself, see – just a quick in an' out job. Still, we got the ruby, and a prisoner. A sneakin' little tamarin! Struggled like anything, gave me a kick in the guts, but after Piebald put the boot in she soon shut up.'

Cheesemite was trembling with rage. But Rio roared with laughter. 'What happened next, friends?'

'We got away, no trouble,' said Piebald. 'Roamer come after us, of course, and we could have blown his ship out of the water, only that poxy wizard went an' spoilt it all by raisin' a storm!'

'Shame!' cried Rio. 'You'd have sunk that sea-mouse easy!'

'We would, friend,' said Piebald quietly. 'And may yet get the chance. Old Gweir mucked up. A schooner put into port this mornin' from the Golden Isles. They'd been cruisin' round, seein' what they could pick up, and what do you think they saw? The *Avenger* itself, bein' worked on by them poxy tamarins while the sea-mice was baskin' in the sunshine! Old Testy kicked that wizard downstairs when he heard about it an' now you can't hardly move outside wivout bumpin' into an Ermine Guard.'

Scratchfur drained his beer and yelled for more. As the mugs arrived, the stoat pulled up a stool and thrust his face so close to Cheesemite's that the little mouse could smell the beery breath. 'Old Testy reckons as how Roamer's in the city right now! He'll try to get the ruby back; and rescue that stinkin' tamarin.'

'He'll have to hurry,' said Piebald, his eyes glittering behind his mask. 'The empress reckons on sacrificing her to the Snake-god at midnight tonight.'

Cheesemite nearly fell off his stool. But Rio shouted with laughter and clapped the two stoats on the back. 'You fellas on leave now?' he asked casually, raising his mug and slurping noisily.

'No chance!' groaned Scratchfur. 'Dawn tomorrer, we sail in the *Night Crow* up to Viperium. Old Testy wants to inspect the fleet – make sure it's ready to sail for Carminel. If everythin's shipshape, we sail in a week!'

Rio raised his mug. 'Here's to victory!'

The stoats cheered, clapped him on the back and drained their mugs in one go. 'Let's go to the 'Pink Dragon' an' have a couple there, then we'll go to the 'Slug and Raven'. You comin', friends? No? Then we'll say g'night!'

As the stoats lurched unsteadily away, Rio

murmured: 'We gotta find the capitano. He gotta know what these devils gonna do with our princess.'

'And about the invasion fleet,' said Cheesemite. 'We'd better get up to the palace, see if we can find –'

There was a sudden commotion by the door, and Captain Blacktail of the Ermine Guard, accompanied by his sergeant, pushed through the crowd and swaggered to the bar. 'By order of Lord Malatesta!' he shouted. 'We have reason to believe that foreign spies are at work in the city. All here will remove their masks!'

Malatesta's guards inspired fear, even in this low tavern where many pirates were gathered. As the customers began pulling off their masks, and the Ermines drew closer to the window, the sea-mice realised that they were only seconds away from capture.

'Out the window, Cheesemite! Now!'

Cheesemite leaped for the sill. But even as he stood, poised for the jump, Captain Blacktail saw him and drew his pistol. A shot rang out. Cheesemite yelped in agony as a bullet flenched his leg and he fell into the cobbled street. Rio vaulted through the window, drew his pistol, and fired into the crowded tavern. Scooping up his wounded friend, Rio flung him over his shoulder, and hurried down the main street before ducking into a side turning. But Captain Blacktail had rounded up some volunteers, they were spilling out of the tavern and the pursuit was closing in. Rio ran down the dark lane and round another corner.

Fleeing through a maze of narrow, twisting alleys, they came at last to a place where derelict houses leaned drunkenly together. Kicking open a door, Rio blundered through darkness to the furthest corner. He listened intently. No sound reached him. He and Cheesemite were safe, for the moment. But his friend was unconscious, his leg was bleeding and Rio knew that the Ermines would not give up until they had run the two sea-mice to earth.

13 Snakes

'Nearly midnight,' said Roamer. 'You'll have a fine view of the lights from up here, Ben!'

'Oi be comin' with you, zur!'

'Not this time. Your job's to lower the rope, with me on the end of it. Unfortunately, the snake-pit lies directly below, so you'll have to swing me away from it so I can jump onto that mosaic path.'

'But suppose the doors are guarded by spiders? We can't see from up here.'

'That's a chance I'll have to take. But I think the room's deserted. All the spiders are guarding the outer doors – I hope! As soon as I'm down, haul up the rope. If I'm not back in an hour, return to the ship by the agreed route. Don't wait for me. *That's an order!'*

Grumbling to himself about his captain's reckless folly, Ben slowly paid out the rope. As Roamer descended, he saw to his relief that the doorways were indeed unguarded. The throne-room was deserted, save for the viper, who was watching the mouse's approach, its tiny forked tongue flickering in the lamplight. When Roamer was level with the pit's edge, Ben began to swing the rope like a pendulum. The viper watched curiously as Roamer swayed across the pit.

Suddenly, the mouse sprang. He landed neatly on the pathway and the rope danced away from him as Ben hauled it up. Unable to see where the mouse had gone, the viper lost interest and went back to sleep.

Roamer crossed the room and stared up at the huge carved snake. It looked much taller from ground level, almost as tall as the *Avenger*'s mizzenmast. From the coils at the base, the body reared up to where emerald eyes glittered in the lamplight. Between the gaping jaws the ruby was glowing softly.

The statue was leaning slightly forwards. Roamer went behind it and saw that although the climb would be steep, it could be done. He climbed swiftly, the ridges that marked the snake's scaly skin giving him plenty of footholds. Ignoring the dizzy height and the hard stone floor below, he arrived at last at the point where the statue's head lunged forward. He was wondering how he was going to reach the ruby, when a rustle of movement from outside the throne-room sent his heart into his mouth.

Roamer flattened himself against the statue's broad, flat head. Peering cautiously down, he saw spiders of the empress's bodyguard scuttle into the throne-room and take up their positions around the walls. Roamer held his breath. Was the great Black Widow herself coming? Since the midnight lights would shortly begin, she should be outside to watch them.

Ravanola swept in and climbed to the centre of her golden web. Luckily for Roamer, the empress, though high above her bodyguards, was still much lower than the statue's head.

'Bring the tamarin!' Roamer's spine tingled. Hearing footsteps directly beneath him, he inched forward. Princess Tamina was standing before the pit. Her paws were not tied. There was no need. She was guarded by two spiders whose smallest bite would kill her.

'You have one minute to live,' purred Ravanola softly and her great web trembled at her power. 'As soon as the midnight lights begin, you will be thrown into the pit where the god-on-earth will slay you. You should feel honoured, my dear. You will be a sacrifice to the Snake-god for the success of my invasion of Carminel.' Ravanola laughed. The web quivered. In the pit, the viper stirred and reared its head.

In the fortress of the Ermine Guard, close to the harbour, Malatesta was listening to Captain Blacktail's report.

'They must've been sea-mice, sir. They shot my sergeant, but I'm sure I winged one of them. We tried to catch them, but they got away.'

'You blundering fool! The city must be crawling with these sea-vermin and you couldn't even capture two of them! Call out the Guard! Get to the palace! Tell any Ermines you see in the streets to follow you! I'll come with you. I don't trust those spiders to catch Roamer. Hurry!'

Captain Blacktail ran from the room, yelling for the Guard. Within minutes, he and Malatesta were leading a strong force of Ermines up the hill, ploughing through the crowded streets, flinging aside stoats and rats. 'Make way, you scum!' screamed Malatesta, hurling rats and stoats out of his way until at last the palace lights loomed above them. 'Come on!' yelled Captain Blacktail. 'We're nearly there!'

Roamer stared in horror. The spiders, their hairy legs hooked round Tamina's arms, had brought her to the very edge of the pit. The viper, his forked tongue flickering, was watching her. Any second now, the midnight lights would begin. Roamer could not imagine what to do. Suddenly, a movement above him made him glance up. He caught his breath. The rope was slowly descending.

Ben was doing the only thing possible. But he could not risk the spiders seeing the rope, so he was paying it out with agonising slowness. Roamer watched as the rope's end drew closer. He and Ben had worked together on many daring expeditions and Roamer guessed what the old sea-mouse was going to do.

As the rope came level with the statue's head, it began to swing. Across the pit, and back towards Roamer. Not quite close enough. Roamer pulled off his mask, stuffed it into his pocket and drew himself into a crouching position. The rope was swinging towards him again and it was now or never because a roar of thunder echoed through the throne-room, dazzling lights flickered across the walls, and Ravanola cried: 'Now!'

Roamer leapt for the rope, caught it and clung on as Ben let it fall – but Roamer was ready for the sickening drop and he clung on with one paw, drawing his pistol with the other.

Ravanola screamed a warning. The two spiders swung round but Roamer was plummeting towards them, pistol blazing. One spider fell screaming into the pit, the other sprang aside. Roamer had a split-second glimpse of Tamina's startled eyes as the rope flew above her. She leapt, and clung on.

As the rope soared to the top of its arc, Roamer thrust the pistol into his belt and started climbing. Tamina was safe for the moment. But he could not leave without the ruby. As the rope swung back towards the statue, Roamer took a flying leap and grabbed the stone jaws. Hanging on with one paw, he reached with the other into the statue's mouth. The ruby was glowing as if in welcome and Roamer plucked it out and thrust it in his pocket as the rope came swinging back.

'Stop them!' Ravanola was beside herself with rage. A spider ran forward and as the rope's end flew across the floor, he reached up with two of his legs, caught the rope and began scrambling up.

Roamer was hanging with one paw from the statue. To jump for the rope was impossible. But Tamina, who had scrambled higher, now wrapped her long tail round the rope and launched herself into mid-air, reaching out her paws. As the rope flew towards the statue, Roamer stretched out his paw, grasped Tamina's and as the rope swung away again, he fired the second barrel of his pistol and the spider who had been climbing towards him screamed and fell.

'Haul away!' yelled Roamer. Out on the rooftop, Ben obeyed. The sky was erupting in starbursts, streaking comets dazzled him, but he ignored the wonderful display, steadily hauling, paw over paw, his eyes fixed on Roamer and the princess. But at the last moment, as the rope began to rise away from her, the furious Ravanola scuttled down from her web, grabbed for the rope and climbed.

Tamina was almost at the top. Roamer was close behind her. But the empress was climbing faster than he was and Roamer could read murder in her eyes.

As Tamina heaved herself onto the rooftop, she gave Ben a swift hug, then helped herself to his pistol. But she could not get a clear shot at Ravanola. To her dismay, she saw that Roamer was still some way from the top and the Black Widow was hard on his heels.

In the palace gardens, the music and dancing stopped abruptly as Malatesta's elite troops charged in. Screams rent the air, chairs went flying, flower-beds were trampled as the Guard tried to force their way through. 'Out of the way, fools!' screamed Malatesta. 'The empress is in danger!'

But when he reached the main entrance, the spider on guard would not let him in. 'No one passes this door without permission from the empress!'

Malatesta glared at him. 'You blithering nincompoop! Don't you understand anything? Get out of my way or the empress will have your head!'

'No.'

'Then I'll kill you myself!' Malatesta's sword glittered in the starlight. One murderous thrust, and the spider fell dead. 'Come on!' yelled Blacktail and led the Guards in a headlong dash into the palace.

His paws aching with the effort of climbing, Roamer at last reached the top. But no sooner had Tamina heaved him clear than a long, black leg appeared. Ben froze in terror. The rope was still tied round his waist and Ravanola was almost on the roof.

'Quick!' yelled Tamina. 'The ruby!'

Roamer fumbled in his pocket. Ravanola scrambled through the skylight. Ignoring Ben, she sped towards Tamina. 'You little wretch!' she hissed. 'You won't escape Ravanola!'

Roamer threw the ruby. Tamina caught it and held it high. A searing burst of blood-red light leapt from its heart. Ravavola screamed as the light burned her eyes. She staggered back, scrabbling blindly for the rope on the edge of the skylight. But Ben had stepped clear and the rope's end was safely in his paws. With a terrible scream, Ravanola fell, straight into the viper's pit. The snake hissed angrily and raised his head to strike as Malatesta's Ermines rushed into the room.

14 The race to the sea

Malatesta's Guards gathered silently round the snake-pit. The spiders gazed in horror at Ravanola's crumpled body. The snake, satisfied after his kill, had coiled up and gone to sleep.

'Sir!' cried Blacktail. 'The ruby's gone!'

'*What*?' Malatesta glared in disbelief at the statue's empty jaws; then he turned his fury on the spiders. 'You blundering fools! Eight legs each and enough poison to slaughter an army and you let that accursed buccaneer get away! I've a good mind to feed you all to the viper!'

Thunderstruck by the death of their empress, the spiders endured his tongue-lashing in silence.

'Look, sir!' Blacktail's sharp eyes had spotted the open skylight. 'That's how they got in!'

'And how they got out! Blacktail, take the troops and scour the city. Start at the top of the hill and work down to the harbour. Cover the side streets as well. Find them!'

As Blacktail and the guards hurried off, Malatesta turned to the spiders. He had humiliated them enough. Now, he wanted to win their loyalty. 'On second thoughts, I will spare your miserable lives. Perhaps you are not entirely to blame. Ravanola must have offended the Snake-god, or he would never have allowed the god-on-earth to kill her. She was childless, the last of her line. From now on, you will obey me. I am Emperor of Salamex!'

In a daze, the spiders bent their front legs and bowed. 'Get that web down,' ordered Malatesta. 'I shan't want it. Cut it up, if you like. Use it for your own webs. I'm going after those sea-mice. When I've caught them, and their precious princess, I'll bring them here and you can have the pleasure of killing them. Slowly.'

That pleased the spiders. Some of them started to

take the web apart while others scuttled off to find a suitable throne for their new emperor.

News of Ravanola's death spread quickly. Though few in the city had ever seen her, the empress was such an awesome presence that it seemed impossible that she could be dead. Suddenly, the carnival was over. Stoats slunk to their houses, rats crept to their dockside hovels or rowed to their ships in the harbour. They did not notice Roamer's cutter, still moored to the quayside.

As Blacktail's Ermines moved relentlessly downhill, searching every shop and tavern, the sea-mice who were waiting on the street corners realised that something had gone wrong. Their task had been to cover Roamer's retreat to the cutter. But Roamer was nowhere to be seen, and to stay at their posts would be to risk capture. Quietly, groups of sea-mice slipped away downhill, following the agreed route that would bring them to the far corner of the harbour where the cutter was waiting, hoping against hope that somehow Roamer would get away and join them.

In the derelict house where Rio and Cheesemite were hiding, Rio noticed the silence, sensed the changed atmosphere. 'Time we go, Cheesemite. You walk, maybe?'

'I'll try.' Despite Rio's bandaging, Cheesemite's leg was so painful that Rio had to support his friend out of the house and down the alley. 'I'm sorry, Rio.'

'Ees no problem! Wadda friends for?'

Suddenly, they heard a rhythmic thudding. 'Ermines,' muttered Rio. 'Tramp, tramp, tramp! They let us know they comin'. Mighty considerate! But we soon get to harbour.'

'I hope they've not captured Captain Roamer.'

'Huh! It take more than a lousy bunch of stoats in fancy cloaks to catch him!'

After descending from the palace roof, Roamer had led Ben and Tamina down the steep slope to the wood. They dared not run for fear of falling and making a noise; with every step, they expected to hear shouts of alarm behind them. But the spiders on guard had all vanished into the palace, and the three friends reached the trees in safety.

The glorious midnight lights had gone. The short summer night would soon be over. Above their heads, a bird chirruped. 'Soon be dawn,' said Roamer. 'We must hurry.'

They trekked through the silent woods until at last they reached a low wall. On the other side was a dingey alley, leading downhill. They scrambled over the wall and crouched in its shadow. 'Stay here,' whispered Roamer. He crept to the corner and peered round.

He saw a wide street. At the far end, fading starlight danced on the water. The harbour! They were almost there! But as he turned to signal to the others, a group of masked figures appeared, running towards him.

Roamer shrank back into the alley and drew his pistol. But as the figures hurried past, Roamer's heart leapt. They wore red strips on their masks! They were his mice!

'*Avengers*!'

'Lord o'Light! It's the captain!'

'Sir! Look out!' Roamer spun round. A troop of Ermines was charging down the street. 'Into those doorways!' snapped Roamer. 'Pistols ready!'

Tamina and Ben had joined him and they all ran for cover on either side of the street. When the Ermines were almost upon them, Roamer yelled: '*Fire*!'

Pistols snapped and three Ermines fell squealing. The others came on, but the sea-mice were armed with double-barrelled weapons and a second volley proved too much for the stoats. They skidded to a halt, turned and fled. But their leader remained. 'If one of you is Roamer,' said Malatesta quietly, 'fight me if you dare.'

Roamer had never seen Malatesta. But he recognised the stoat lord by the famous spike where his left paw used to be. Helping himself to a fallen stoat's sword, he said: 'I'm Roamer. Keep back, the rest of you. This is between Malatesta and me.'

15 The poisoned spike

Roamer knew he had to be quick. More guards might come along at any moment. He ran at Malatesta, swinging his sword in a cut for the head, but the stoat parried easily and lunged for Roamer's heart. Roamer swept the sword aside and thrust for a kill. Again, the stoat parried, returned to the attack and Roamer leaped clear as the spike came flashing down.

Tired after his night's adventures, Roamer was finding it hard to concentrate on his enemy's sword and spike at the same time. Suddenly, the stoat swung back his sword for a cut. Roamer lunged and though Malatesta jumped clear, Roamer's sword had nicked his side and blood was trickling to the ground. The stoat snarled, attacked again, cutting and lunging until his sword and Roamer's were locked together at the hilt. Roamer was at Malatesta's mercy for the spike was raised for a kill, but Roamer slammed his fist into Malatesta's jaw and the stoat collapsed.

'Kill him!' cried Tamina.

'He's helpless. Out cold. I can't kill him.'

'Huh! He'd kill you soon enough if you were helpless!'

'He probably would. But I'm not him. Now let's go.'

They ran to the end of the street, swung right and dashed along the quayside. Other mice were running for the cutter, several were already aboard and they cheered as they spotted Roamer and Tamina. But the shooting in the side street had alerted Captain Blacktail. Already he was leading his troop down the main street in a dash for the quayside.

'Is everyone here?' Roamer was peering at the crew, who were hoisting the sail and pulling out the oars.

'Rio an' Cheesemite ain't here, Skipper!'

'Captain! Ermines to starb'd! At the far end of the dockside!'

'Pistols ready, lads!'

'Look, zur! *Rio an' Cheesemite*!'

They had emerged from an alley, midway between the cutter and the Ermines. 'Come on!' yelled the crew. But Rio was almost exhausted with the effort of supporting Cheesemite. He was going as fast as he could but the Ermines had seen him and were gaining on him.

'Starboard crew, stand by!' roared Roamer. 'Give 'em a broadside! Fire!'

A dozen pistols flamed. Some of the Ermines fell, but Blacktail urged the rest on. As Rio staggered up to the cutter, Cheesemite slipped from his grasp. He limped towards the charging soldiers, levelled his pistol and fired.

Blacktail fell, screaming, a bullet in his leg. As the Ermines checked, and clustered round their fallen leader, Cheesemite hobbled to the cutter and cheering mice hauled him aboard. With a single swipe of his cutlass, Ben sliced the mooring rope, the mice bent to the oars and the cutter surged away from the quayside.

'Shoot them, you fools!' yelled Blacktail, furious with rage and pain, and the mice ducked as a volley crashed out and bullets flew overhead. Suddenly, a heavy cannon boomed across the water. The *Avenger* was sailing to the rescue.

The mice cheered. But Tamina was looking anxiously at Roamer. 'What's the matter?'

Roamer could not understand why he was feeling so ill. 'I don't know. Just tired, I expect.' But it was worse than that. Through waves of dizziness, he noticed a rip in his sleeve and a faint trickle of blood.

When they reached the ship, Roamer managed to clamber up the rope ladder. But once on deck, he collapsed. While the anxious crew set sail and Lukas steered the ship out of the harbour, Rio, Ben and Tamina knelt beside the captain.

'He didn't take no wound,' said Ben. But Tamina had heard about Malatesta's poisoned spike and when she spotted the rip in Roamer's sleeve, she said: 'It must have happened when Malatesta fell. Get me a bucket of seawater. Quickly! *Or he'll die!*'

As Rio ran for the water, Tamina ripped away Roamer's sleeve. The wound had dried, so she gently touched her dagger to it until the blood flowed. Then, she sucked the poisoned blood, spat it over the side and rinsed her mouth with the seawater. Again and again she returned to the wound until at last the foul taste of the poison had gone. She bandaged the wound, cleaned her dagger and replaced it in her boot. 'Now all we can do is wait.'

As the ship sped on, mice stood silent in the

rigging or sat tensely on the deck. All watched Roamer. 'His heart is scarcely beating,' said Tamina. 'But there's nothing more we can do.'

Dawn was breaking and golden sunlight was flooding the ship when at last Roamer opened his eyes. 'What happened? Did we get away? Tamina, why are you crying?'

'You were hurt, but you're better now. We all got away, thanks to you.' She scuffed the tears away. 'And I'm not crying!'

In the throne-room of the House of the Snake, a tall, brown-robed stoat was standing in a shaft of sunshine that beamed down from the skylight. The rest of the room was in darkness, especially around Malatesta's new throne, where the shadows clustered thickly.

'I have come to pledge my loyalty,' said Gweir.

'Huh! Where were you when I needed you?' Malatesta's head was throbbing painfully after his fall, and he was furious at the buccaneers' escape.

'Praying to the Snake-god to spare the empress's life.'

'That was a waste of time!' As Malatesta rose from the throne, Gweir felt his flesh creep. Deep shadows were following the new emperor, twisting and turning like snakes at his heels.

'That accursed buccaneer's got the ruby,' hissed Malatesta. 'But this morning, I sail for the port of Viperium. Soon I shall lead the fleet to Carminel. We shall no doubt overtake Roamer's ship on the way, and destroy it. You'd better come too. I might need some magic. Now get out of here.'

Gweir fled. Empress Ravanola had been cold-hearted and cruel; but Malatesta, Lord of Shadows, was pure evil. The mice of Carminel, thought Gweir, were surely doomed.

16 Raven

'Deck, there!' High in the crosstrees, Cheesemite was squeaking with excitement. 'Strange sail ahead!'

Roamer sprang into the rigging and trained his telescope on the distant ship. Princess Tamina scowled. 'I wish you'd stop leaping about. That wound hasn't healed yet.'

But Roamer had never felt better, and after hearing from Rio and Cheesemite about the invasion fleet at Viperium, he was eager for action!

'Blimey!' yelled Cheesemite. 'It's the *Raven*!'

'The treasure-ship!' cried Lukas. 'But why would she be heading for Viperium?'

'To join the invasion fleet,' said Roamer, jumping back to the quarterdeck and ignoring Tamina's cross face. 'She's a big ship, useful for carrying soldiers. Hoist top-gallants and royals! We'll catch her, and if there's treasure aboard we'll help ourselves!'

Avenger still wore her disguise. If the *Raven*'s sea-rats spotted her, they would think she was another of Malatesta's ships. All that afternoon, they followed the treasure-ship and were rapidly closing the distance when Cheesemite shouted: 'Land ahead!'

The sea-mice craned over the side or scrambled into the rigging, gazing eagerly at the long, curving coastline of Salamex. Away to the right, burning plains ended in shingle beaches; to the left, a high hill, like an island and crowned with a fort, jutted from the land. Between the hill and the beach lay the broad mouth of a river. The treasure-ship had anchored there, just below the fort.

'Take in sail!' snapped Roamer.

'Why's she anchored there?' wondered Lukas.

'The tide's running strongly away from the coast,' said Roamer. 'Probably that river's not deep enough for the *Raven*. She must wait until high tide before venturing in. The port of Viperium's certainly well protected; a river that's only safe at high tide and that hilltop fort! See its guns? Lukas, we must anchor; make the sea-rats think we're waiting for the tide as well. Then, when it's dark, we'll give them a little surprise. First, supper. I'm going to my cabin to make plans.'

While the mice supped on hot soup and chunks of bread, Roamer pondered the problem. To capture the *Raven*, he would have to capture the fort as well. For an hour he sat lost in thought, now and then absent-mindedly nibbling a nut. At last, he knew how it could be done. Calling to Lukas to wake him in an hour's time, he stretched out on his bunk and fell asleep.

At nightfall, *Avenger* weighed anchor and slipped away up the coast, with the fort on its tall headland to starboard. The mice kept still and silent. Sound travels far at night and if the stoats in the fort heard them, their adventure would be over before it had begun.

'Lukas, take her as close in as you dare,' Roamer said quietly. 'Then drop anchor. Ben, get ready to launch the cutter. You all know what to do. Good luck!'

There was no moon and clouds covered the stars. Lukas, who was to remain behind with some of the crew, had anchored the ship opposite a small cove and the sea-mice rowed ashore with muffled oars. As the cutter grated on the sand, twelve of the mice jumped out and followed Roamer up the steep hillside. The cutter returned to the *Avenger*, where Tamina's group was waiting.

The hillside was thick with spiky bushes, so there was plenty of cover. As the fort loomed above them, the mice saw stoats staring seawards from the battlements, unaware that a force of buccaneers was creeping up the slope. As Roamer drew near to the summit, he changed direction and led his mice round the hill until they reached the rear of the fort. Now, they could see the river and the *Raven*'s masts. 'No sentries here,' whispered Roamer. 'They're all looking out to sea. Let's get into position. Keep under cover. Move slowly. We've plenty of time.'

Tamina, meanwhile, was leading her mice round the base of the hill. They crept silently through the bushes until they saw the *Raven*, moored to a small landing-stage. 'No guards,' breathed Rio. 'Them sea-rats got no brains at all!'

'They think they're safe under the fort's guns,' whispered Tamina. 'But they're in for a nasty shock.' She gathered her mice around her. Their eyes were shining. Cheesemite was especially excited. His wound had healed and he was eager for adventure. Tamina whispered: 'You see the path that runs from the landing-stage, uphill through the bushes to the fort? Take up your positions on either side of it. Then wait until I give the word.'

Captain Foultail of the *Raven* was snoring peacefully in his bunk. It had been a prosperous voyage. He and his sea-rats had plundered the Golden Isles to their hearts' content; crates of gold and caskets of jewels lay snugly in the hold. Suddenly, Captain Foultail was rudely awakened by a burst of firing and a voice from the shore yelling: 'Help! The fort's being attacked!'

Foultail hurtled out of bed, dragged on his boots and groped for his sword and pistols. As the rest of the crew burst on deck, all armed to the teeth, they could see that the fort was surrounded with flashes of gunfire. 'Help!' yelled the voice again. 'We're bein' attacked! It's that pirate, Roamer an' his devil-mice!'

'Roamer?' roared Foultail. 'You hear that, mates? Malatesta's put a price of fifty thousand gold pieces on that mouse's head, dead or alive! Let's go an' get 'im!' Yelling wildly at the prospect of yet more riches, the rats flooded off the ship, thundered across the landing-stage and up the zigzag path. As they climbed the hill, the sound of firing grew louder and flashes along the fort's wall showed where the stoats were firing back. 'Come on!' screamed Foultail and his the rats charged after him, firing their pistols into the air and whooping with excitement.

Up on the battlements, Fangast, the stoat commander, peered nervously into the darkness. He was totally bewildered by the sudden outburst of firing, and had no idea who was attacking him. All he could see were flashes of gunfire from the bushes. Now, up the path came the sea-rats, firing their pistols and yelling like fury. Convinced that more enemies were attacking, Fangast yelled: 'Aim for the path! Fire!'

As his rats began to scream and fall, the terrible truth dawned on Captain Foultail: Roamer's mice must have taken the fort! What an honour it would be, he thought, for his rats to recapture it! 'Come on, you lousy scumbags!' he bawled. 'Up to the walls! Kill them mice! Aim for the flashes of gunfire!'

The battle raged on. Many stoats screamed and toppled from the ramparts. Many rats fell squealing. At last, the firing from the bushes died away and a coarse voice cried: 'Ahoy, there!'

'Who is that?' Fangast called nervously from the battlements.

'Why, your friends from the *Raven*, o'course!' came the reply, followed by a gust of bloodcurdling laughter. 'That pirate, Roamer, caught you stoats nappin' good an' proper! But thanks to us, him an' his mice are dead, rot their souls! Open the gate, friend, and let us in!'

'Do as he says!' cried Fangast in relief. 'Lord Malatesta shall hear of this,' he said, as his stoats flung open the gate, 'specially if you've killed that accursed Roamer, though me an' my stoats should have a share of the prize money . . . Hey! Just a minute! You ain't sea-rats! Shut the gate!'

But it was too late. Roamer's mice, pistols blazing, were charging into the courtyard. So furious and unexpected was this sudden attack, that the stoats flung down their weapons and surrendered. Fangast found himself disarmed and his paws lashed behind his back. 'What's goin' on?' he demanded. 'I thought you was sea-rats!'

'That was what we wanted you to think,' said Roamer with a cheerful smile. 'There *were* sea-rats, a while ago, who came up the path to help you. Your stoats killed most of them, and here come the rest! Sorry-looking bunch, aren't they?'

Escorted by Tamina's mice, the few survivors of the *Raven*'s crew were dragging themselves miserably through the gateway. They looked as bewildered as the stoats.

Old Ben was wheezing with laughter. 'That were the best fight I ever been in, by thunder if it weren't! Stoats shootin' rats, rats shootin' stoats – and us, a-crawlin' through the bushes, knockin' them rats on the head an' trussin' them up, an' every so often takin' a pot shot at the wall! Don't know when I've enjoyed meself so much!'

'Get the prisoners to the dungeons,' said Roamer. 'Give them food, water and bandages. They can look after themselves until Malatesta finds them and lets them out, though I'd not like to be in their shoes when he does!'

When the courtyard was clear of prisoners, and the mice were gorging themselves on plundered bread, cheese and baked potatoes, Roamer asked: 'How many of our mice were hurt, Ben?'

'None that I knows of. A great victory, zur!'

'It was brilliant!' Tamina's eyes were shining. 'You should have heard Cheesemite down on the landing-stage. He completely fooled those rats, and led them up the path, yelling that the mice were attacking!'

'What we do now, Capitano?' asked Rio.

'Send word to Lukas. We've a night's work ahead.

At dawn tomorrow, we attack Malatesta's fleet in the harbour of Viperium!'

17 Hellburner

At first light, while Tamina and a force of buccaneers stayed behind to hold the captured fort, *Avenger* and *Raven* glided upriver.

Aboard the captured ship, now empty of treasure, Rio was loading the guns with double-shot and laying gunpowder trails to where Cheesemite was building a pile of rags, spare sails and bits of the rats' spare clothing. Ben was deep in the hold, lashing powder-casks together. When they had finished, the mice gathered in the bows and signalled to Roamer. It was not a moment too soon, for the river was widening, and the harbour of Viperium lay before them.

'Lord o' Light!' exclaimed Lukas. 'I never seen so many ships!' Several were lying at anchor, many others were moored in a long line to the quayside. Slowly, the *Avenger* glided in. The *Raven* was some distance to starboard, a small rowing boat moored to her side. At Roamer's signal, both ships dropped anchor. 'It's a terrible thing we're going to do, skipper,' said Lukas grimly.

'I know. But if Carminel is to be saved, this fleet must be destroyed, or at least damaged so badly that Malatesta won't be able to bring as many stoats as he'd have liked. But I don't like it any more than you do.'

'Look, skipper!' Lukas was pointing skywards. Vultures were circling above the harbour. 'Just as well you posted sharpshooters.'

'Aye, and netting across the upper deck. But there'll be no protection for you and me.'

Lukas grinned. 'We'll survive! Look, Ben and the others are ready. Shall we start?'

He waved across to the *Raven*. Rio and Cheesemite clambered into the rowing-boat and made ready to cast off. Aboard *Avenger*, all eyes were on the *Raven*. Suddenly, a tiny flame blossomed on her upper

131

deck. Old Ben appeared at the siderail, gave a cheery wave, and climbed down to the boat. At the same moment, Rio hacked through the *Raven*'s anchor cable with three mighty blows of his cutlass. By the time the mice were safely aboard *Avenger*, the fire which Ben had started had reached the *Raven*'s rigging and she was sailing straight for a gap between two enemy ships. The *Raven* had been turned into a gigantic firework; and any moment now . . .

Suddenly, her double-shotted guns exploded with a deafening roar and shattering broadsides slammed into the enemy ships. Splinters flew, gaping holes appeared in their sides, and as terrified rats dived overboard and swam for their lives, the two mighty ships keeled over and sank.

The *Raven* sailed on, more guns exploding, flames licking up the rigging, snaking up the masts and out along the spars to turn the black sails red before devouring them. Panic-stricken rats were cutting their cables, but as the fire aboard *Raven* reached the lower deck, another broadside roared across the harbour and ships flinched and groaned as the huge weight of flying metal struck home.

The ship was now a pillar of fire. 'She's almost at the quayside,' muttered Lukas. 'Now!' With a rending crash, the *Raven* struck the line of warships. Instantly, the fire leaped from her spars to attack the ships alongside, which burst into flame and ignited those on either side. Several sea-rats managed to sail their ships out of danger, but the fire aboard *Raven* was still blazing hungrily. At last, it found the powder barrels.

With a thunderous roar, the ship exploded, guns, masts, spars flying into the air. When the noise had died away, all the mice could hear were the yells of the furious sea-rats and the frantic squawking of the terrified vultures. But there was no time to waste. From far off to the right, a tall ship, all sails set, was racing towards them. Lukas was the first to spot it. He recognised it at once. 'Skipper, look out! The *Night Crow*!'

'Cut the anchor cable!' snapped Roamer. 'Make more sail! We can't fight Malatesta here, there's not enough space and we have to get back to the fort for Tamina. Lukas, turn the ship round!'

'There's no time!' Lukas was spinning the wheel, the ship, heavy with treasure, was turning with painful slowness and the *Night Crow* was almost upon them.

'Port-side guns, stand by!' roared Roamer. His mice were ready, staring through the open gunports at the approaching enemy. 'We'll give her a broadside! Fire!'

The *Avenger* shuddered as her guns flamed and roared. Splinters flew from the *Night Crow*'s bows, holes appeared in her sails and the mice cheered as the top section of her foremast vanished in a shower of splinters. As the *Avenger* completed her turn, mice leaped to haul the sails round to catch the wind. Guns were firing from the *Night Crow*, but the cannonballs fell harmlessly into the water, for the *Avenger* was clear, and sailing for the river-mouth. As the banks closed in, the ship seemed to fly along. But something strange was happening. Aboard the *Night Crow*, sea-rats were taking in sails. The ship was slowing. 'They're giving up the chase!' yelled Lukas.

'Why would they do that?' asked Roamer. 'Our guns hardly touched them.' High in the crosstrees, Cheesemite's sharp eyes had spotted the reason, a worse peril even than Malatesta. 'Captain! *Vultures*!'

Beyond the *Night Crow*, a flock of huge birds was rapidly approaching. As they drew closer, the mice could see stoats perched on their backs. Their cloaks were flying in the wind, they were yelling and waving their swords. The vultures flew low over the *Avenger*, streaked down the river, then climbed into the sky.

'Aren't they goin' to attack?' muttered Lukas.

'They're gaining height,' said Roamer. 'They're going to charge down on us. That's why Malatesta's slowing down. He's leaving room for them. Sharpshooters! Stand by! *Here they come!*'

18 Vulture attack

'Ben, take the wheel,' said Roamer calmly. 'Lukas and I will cover you. You mice on the deck, keep your heads down! Sharpshooters, fire when you like!'

In arrowhead formation, the vultures were swooping lower. Perched astride the leader, Captain Blacktail was flying straight for a group of frightened-looking mice. They were clustered together in the foremast's 'fighting top'. This was a large, basket-shaped structure, just below the topsail. Blacktail was aiming his pistol and was about to pull the trigger when the mice suddenly raised their hidden rifles, took split-second aim and fired.

As a bullet zinged over his head, Blacktail saw several rats toppling from their vultures, and one screeching bird plummeting to the water. As the mice in the mainmast fighting top fired as well, Blacktail's vulture swerved aside and the rest followed, the cheers of the sea-mice echoing in their ears.

'We showed 'em, eh, Cheesemite?' grinned Rio.

Cheesemite had descended from his perch to join his friends in the fighting top. He grinned broadly. 'Yeah, we showed 'em, Rio! Them ugly great birds won't come back in a hurry – oh, Lord o'Light, Rio, *here they come again*!'

Blacktail was flying in from the starboard side, his stoats aiming their pistols at all three fighting tops at once. Two vultures, more daring than the rest, flew low between the masts and Cheesemite flinched as a long, vicious beak and massive, hooked talons streaked past him. A hail of bullets struck the fighting top and Cheesemite staggered back, over-balanced and fell.

A rush of air in his ears, a black blur as he flew past the billowing sail – then his claws fastened on a dangling rope. As he came to a sudden stop, the shock nearly finished him, but he clung on, swaying wildly, the excited cheering of his friends above coming dimly to his ears.

When his heart had ceased pounding quite so loudly, Cheesemite clambered up the rope until he emerged onto the platform in the middle of the fighting top. 'Where you been, Cheesemite?' grinned Rio.

'I just popped out for a moment,' replied Cheesemite, rather shakily.

Rio gave a delighted bellow of laughter. 'Well, I'm sure glad you decided to poppa back! You just in time, li'l pal. Here come them stinkin' vultures again!'

Blacktail was getting desperate. He knew Malatesta was counting on him to kill the sea-mice. So far he had not even injured one, but had lost several rats and at least two vultures. Now he changed his tactics. He signalled with his sword and the well-drilled stoats swung their vultures into a new formation. 'Oh-oh,' muttered Rio. 'I sure don't like the look of this.'

The vultures had flown back along the river until they were well astern of both ships. Now, they wheeled, circled and split into two groups, one on either side of the river. 'They're going to attack from both sides at once,' muttered Lukas.

'To confuse our fire,' said Roamer. 'If it works, they'll try it again, next time from our front. By that time, we should be almost level with the fort . . . I know what we'll do!'

Roamer gave a piercing whistle. At once, two mice ducked beneath the netting and climbed to the quarterdeck. 'Take our rifles,' said Roamer. 'Make sure Ben doesn't end up as vulture meat. Lukas, come with me. We're going to fire the carronade!'

Ducking below the netting, Lukas followed Roamer to the bows. There was the squat, ugly cannon known as the carronade, its stubby barrel pointing out at an angle to the deck. 'Not much use at long range,' muttered Roamer. 'But devastating in close action. And we can raise it much higher than the other guns. Help me with the levers.'

Together, they struggled to raise the short barrel until it was pointing upwards. 'Now lever it round! We want it pointing forward . . . Look out, here they come!'

Vultures were flying in single file on both sides, the stoats firing in turn as they drew level with the ship. Several cries from the fighting tops showed that some bullets had hit their mark. When the vultures had passed, shouts came from the masts. 'Captain! We're almost out of ammunition!'

Far ahead, the vultures were turning for another attack. Lukas was hastily ramming powder and shot into the carronade; it did not fire ordinary cannonballs, but big, exploding shells. As the vultures came swooping down again, Roamer touched the slow match to the big gun and jumped aside as the carronade thundered. 'Look at that!'

The shell exploded with a shattering roar. Several vultures fell with a mighty splash, the others wheeled away in panic. But only one line had been hit. The other was still flying; and the mice had nothing left to fire at it.

From the fort's gun-platform, high above the river, Princess Tamina and her buccaneers had been anxiously watching for the *Avenger*. They had loaded the big cannons, in case Roamer needed help. For some time, they had heard firing, and had seen the clouds of vultures; now, at last, they saw the *Avenger*, and heard the carronade's roar.

'Here they come!' yelled Tamina.

'Look, Princess! Them vultures is getting ready for another charge!'

'We can stop them!' yelled Tamina. 'Fire!' Six cannons thundered. By the time their deafening roar had died away, four more vultures had plummeted to the water. In despair, Blacktail broke off the attack. The *Avenger*, clear of the river, was sailing out to the open sea.

'Where's he going?' demanded Tamina. 'Has he forgotten about us?'

'Look, Princess!' yelled one of the buccaneers. 'There's a Salamex warship – hanged if it ain't the *Night Crow*! The skipper ain't forgotten us; he's gettin' ready to fight! The wind's blowin' *towards* us. See how *Avenger*'s tiltin' over to the wind? Skipper'll wait till he's got enough searoom, then he'll turn, so he can attack the *Night Crow* with the wind behind him.'

'Ar,' said another mouse. 'He be gettin' the weather gauge, y'see. That's what it's called, the weather gauge. Now, if he hadn't –'

'That's all jolly interesting,' said Tamina. 'But shouldn't we be getting back to the cutter? As soon as Roamer's dealt with the *Night Crow*, he can pick us up.'

'Ar,' said the mouse. 'That might take a while. Nasty big ship, the *Night Crow*. Especially if that old varmint Mal'testy's aboard!'

19 The cannons' roar

'I think we've got enough searoom now,' said Roamer cheerfully. 'Bring her round, Lukas, so that we have the wind behind us. Then we can do whatever we like.'

Lukas spun the wheel and the *Avenger*, which had been tilting steeply, swung gracefully round. 'Take in sail,' shouted Roamer. 'I don't want to fly past him; I want time to sink the varmint!' The crew laughed and the *Avenger* sailed slowly towards the now distant river-mouth, the fort and the *Night Crow*.

'Action stations!' called Roamer. 'All guns to load

with double-shot! Load the carronades! Cheesemite, come down from the crosstrees and help Rio on the lower gundeck.'

Cheesemite felt relieved not to be spending the battle high above it. He slid down a rope, landed on the deck and called: 'Captain, sir! Shall I hoist our colours?'

Roamer had forgotten that the dead empress's flag still waved from his topmast. 'Thanks, Cheesemite! Haul down that foul spider's rag and run up our own flag!'

As the Royal Banner of Carminel rose to the masthead, the sea-mice cheered and when Roamer drew his sword and shouted: 'King Caladon and victory!' they cheered even louder.

But as they drew closer to the enemy, the buccaneers fell silent. The guns were ready and the smell of slow-burning matches lay heavy on the air. The only sound was the creaking of the rigging. As Cheesemite crept along the lower gundeck, he felt the butterflies dancing in his stomach and a sick feeling rising in his throat.

Cheesemite and Rio crouched in the semi-darkness beside their long cannon. Through the open gunport, all they could see was the water flowing by but they knew that in a few minutes they would see the enemy and hear the crash of guns. Cheesemite gulped. 'Rio! I'm scared!'

Rio put his arm round his trembling friend. 'Sure you are! And I let you into a secret; I scared too!'

Cheesemite was astonished. 'You are?'

'Sure I am! We all are, even the capitano. You's in good company, Cheesemite. But it'll be all right. Rio will look after you.'

Cheesemite felt better. 'Sure, Rio. We'll look after each other, shall we?'

Roamer's eyes were fixed on the *Night Crow*. With the wind against her, and her sails hauled hard round, Malatesta's ship was leaning steeply. 'Her lower gundeck must be awash,' said Lukas. 'Shall we attack her on that side?'

'No. We'll pass down the *other* side, to starboard. Her guns will be pointing upwards and may do some damage to our masts and rigging. But with her hull tilting so much, we can get in a broadside *below her waterline*.'

Aboard *Night Crow*, the tilt was so steep that Malatesta was clinging to the rail. He glared at Mouldcrust, the sea-rat who was steering. 'Can't we go any faster, curse you?'

Mouldcrust shook his head. 'Not with the wind against us, m'lord.'

144

Malatesta ground his teeth. He was furious with Blacktail and the vultures and was wishing he had brought Gweir along to work some magic. But now the *Avenger* was looming larger. She would soon be level with the *Night Crow*. 'Stand by to fire!' screamed Malatesta. 'Sink that cursed pirate, do you hear me? Kill every mouse aboard! But take Roamer and that meddling tamarin alive. And I've a hundred gold pieces for the rat who finds the ruby!'

Cheesemite was staring through the gunport. Suddenly, the enemy hull was alongside, streaking past with cannons blazing! The ships were so close that Cheesemite could see the rats behind their gunports and he flinched from the dazzling flashes and deafening roar.

'Fire!' At Roamer's command, *Avenger*'s guns thundered in reply. Rio yelled: 'Now we show them rats who's boss, Cheesemite!' Powder-smoke billowed along the gundeck; there was no more time to be scared. Deafened by the cannons' roar, mice were sponging out their guns and ramming more powder and shot into those smoking mouths before running out the guns and firing again.

Malatesta felt his ship reel. But his guns had done some damage and he grinned savagely as the top of

Avenger's foremast vanished, sails and rigging crashing to the deck. 'There goes her main topmast, too!' he shrieked triumphantly. 'We've won! Let's ram them and board them and kill them all! *Avenger*'s finished!'

'No, she ain't,' muttered Mouldcrust mutinously.

'What was that?' snarled Malatesta.

Mouldcrust had been in more sea-fights than he could remember and he knew that Malatesta was leading them all to disaster. 'We've not hit their hull, though they've hit us good an' proper!' he said angrily. 'Two dozen cannon balls on the waterline! You think we can survive that? And still them mice are firin'! Now see what they're doin'!'

'What?' snapped Malatesta.

'Crossin' behind us, same as I'd do if I had the wind behind me!' Mouldcrust was right. *Avenger* had sailed clear past her enemy. Now, she was turning, ready to cross the *Night Crow*'s stern. Suddenly, Malatesta caught sight of Roamer, standing, like him, on his ship's quarterdeck. The stoat lord seized a rifle, rested it along the rail and took careful aim.

As *Avenger* swung into the turn, Roamer yelled: 'Port-side carronade! You've only one shot, so make it a good one!'

The mice at the carronade grinned and waved. As

the *Night Crow*'s high stern loomed above them, they fired. At the same moment, Malatesta pulled the trigger.

It was the flash of sunlight on the spike that alerted Lukas. But his warning shout was drowned by the carronade's roar. He flung himself on Roamer and they both crashed to the deck.

Aboard *Night Crow*, the rats were yelling in terror. The carronade's shell had smashed along the whole length of the ship. The mainmast was toppling, spars, sails and rigging were tumbling to the deck. Malatesta was raving and screaming: 'Fire back, curse you!' But it was too late. Beneath the bows, the shell exploded with an almighty crash, rats jumped for their lives, the whole ship took a sickening lurch and the hungry sea flooded in.

Roamer staggered to his feet, wondering what had knocked him over. Realising that his mice were cheering, he peered through the choking powder-smoke. The *Night Crow* was tilting forward, higher and higher until she was upright in the water. Then, with a groan and a shudder, she slid beneath the waves.

'We did it, Lukas!' cried Roamer. 'We did it . . .' But Lukas did not reply. Roamer fell to his knees beside the still body. He took Lukas's paw. The crew still shouted and cheered for a great victory. But for Roamer, there could be no joy or excitement. His dearest friend lay dead.

As the sea-mice realised what had happened, the cheering died away. 'It were Malatesta what killed him,' said Old Ben, the tears coursing down his fur. 'I saw him fire. I reckon he were aimin' at you.'

'And Lukas pushed me out of the way. He died to save my life.' Roamer ran to the rail and stared at the water, which was swarming with rats, all swimming for the shore. Several vultures were swooping to pick them up, though the birds kept well clear of the *Avenger*. 'Shall we shoot 'em, zur?' asked Ben.

'No. The rats fought bravely, they deserve to be saved. *But I want Malatesta*!'

For a long time, the mice scanned the water. But there was no sign of the stoat lord. 'He must have gone down with his ship, zur. But there's the cutter, wi' our princess!'

'Get her and the others aboard, Ben. Then set course for the Golden Isles. We'll spend the winter there. Even if Malatesta's survived, he can't invade Carminel before the spring. Besides, our poor old *Avenger*'s so battered I don't think she'd survive the long voyage home . . . Look! What's that, floating in the water?'

'That, zur, is the rear section of the *Night Crow*. There's the rails, see, and you can just read the name. All that's left of ol' Mal'testy, I reckons! Shall us fish it out for a souvenir?'

'No! It'd bring us bad luck. Leave it to rot . . .'

For the rest of that day, the tide was kept busy washing bits of wreckage onto the beach below the fort. Last to arrive was the section of *Night Crow* that Roamer had spotted in the water. If only he had fished it out, or even inspected it more closely, the future would have been very different. For a long time, it lay on the beach. Then, as snake-like shadows began to weave around it, it moved. Someone was crawling out from under it, and the sunlight gleamed on a spike.

Slowly, Malatesta rose to his feet, the shadows clustering about him. He raised hate-filled eyes to the horizon, where the *Avenger's* sails were still visible. 'Curse you, Roamer. I thought I had killed you, but I heard you insult me as I lay in the water. You have wrecked my plans, burned half my fleet, sunk my ship. But I shall repair my fleet, I shall invade Carminel. I shall destroy its cities, I shall burn its farms, I shall slaughter every mouse that lives. But above all, Roamer, I shall destroy you!'

PART THREE
THE CASTLE IN THE CLOUDS

20 Marengo

'Eat, my gallant Lancers!' cried Captain Balbi. 'Drink your fill! It's all free!'

With a rousing cheer and roars of laughter, fifty Red Lancers surged towards the long trestle tables and fell upon the heaped plates and jugs of foaming ale. Never had there been such a feast! Huge pies stuffed with apples, dates and walnuts; blackberry tarts smothered in cream; baked potatoes dripping with melted butter and cheese; a massive dish of cod, tuna and hake, fresh from the harbour and roasted with the most exotic spices the Vittles Lane merchants could provide.

At one end of the long hall, a huge log fire kept the winter cold at bay. But the room was so crowded with soldiers that the warmth did not reach as far as the other end, where Spital, Chowdmouse and the other orphans huddled together. Now that they were almost fully grown, their ragged clothes were too small for them, and they were shivering.

'This was supposed to be our feast,' muttered Chowdmouse, gazing hungrily at the swaggering Lancers, who were stuffing themselves with food and pouring ale down their throats.

'This was supposed to be our house,' sighed Spital. 'The cardinal bought it for us with Princess Tamina's gold. Now the Red Duke's stolen it as a home for his Red Lancers, and we're worse off than before.'

'Yeah. We 'ave to slave for them soldiers. Can't even live with the cardinal no more since he was put in prison.'

'For sticking up for Captain Roamer,' said Spital in disgust, 'when Duke Flambeau declared him a traitor for kidnapping the king.'

'But Caladon weren't kidnapped. He's safe away with the beavers and when he comes back we're goin' to be his bodyguard, remember?'

'If he comes back,' said Spital gloomily. 'Winter's

nearly over, though it's still perishin' cold! But no sign of Caladon.'

A sudden gust of wind whistled round their feet as the door was edged open. Cranberry sidled in. He too had grown since that evening when he and his friends had escorted Caladon aboard the beavers' schooner. But like his father, the landlord of the 'King's Head', Cranberry had grown outwards rather than upwards. He hurried over to his friends, a cloth-wrapped bundle in his arms. 'I've brought you some food,' he whispered. 'My father said to bring it. He hates the duke and the Red Lancers. Trouble is, they've got guns and nobody else has.'

'Yeah, we all 'ave to do as the Red Duke says,' muttered Spital. 'He's power mad, he is.'

Chowdmouse was unwrapping the bundle. 'Cor, thanks, Cranberry,' he whispered. 'Look, fellas, cheese pies, apples an' oranges!'

'What's that?' shouted a harsh voice. The mice looked up in alarm. Captain Balbi was glaring down at them. 'Where has this little feast sprung from, hmmm?'

None of the mice spoke. Balbi grinned. 'You're name's Cranberry, isn't it? From the 'Duke's Head'?'

Cranberry nodded. He felt deeply ashamed that his father had changed the famous old inn's name.

But one night, a group of drunken Red Lancers had threatened to burn the inn to the ground unless he did so.

'Bringing food to these snivelling orphans, are you?' sneered Balbi as several grinning Lancers gathered round. 'We can't have that, can we? They'll soon be as fat as you! What shall we do with this naughty little mouse?'

'Slit his ears!' yelled a Lancer.

'Roast him over the fire!' shouted another.

'Good idea,' said Balbi. 'Grab him!'

Cranberry punched Balbi squarely on the snout. As the Captain reeled back, blood spurting, Spital lashed out with his foot and a Red Lancer fell squealing, while Chowdmouse threw himself on the ground and bit another soldier's ankle.

But it was no use. The young mice were overpowered and two burly Lancers grabbed Cranberry and dragged him to the fire.

'I'll teach you not to strike the commander of the Duke's Guard!' snarled Balbi. 'Roast the little beast until he squeals!'

'Do what you want!' yelled Cranberry. 'You won't hear me beg for mercy, you thievin' scum!'

Suddenly, an icy blast swept down the hall and in strode a tall mouse. Though his thick grey fur was flecked with white, he carried himself like a warrior. He was dressed in a warm coat and woollen leggings and his scarlet cloak was thrown open to show the jewelled hilt of his rapier. Behind him came twenty or more armed mice, all dressed in colourful coats.

'What's going on here?' asked the tall mouse quietly.

'Who are you?' demanded Balbi.

For answer, the grey-furred mouse drew his rapier and held it to Balbi's throat. 'I asked you a question. Now let that mouse go!'

'We were only having a bit of f-fun!' stammered Balbi nervously.

'I said, *let him go*!' As the soldiers hurriedly released Cranberry, the stranger's followers drew their pistols and pointed them at the Red Lancers. Though they outnumbered the newcomers, the duke's mice were glancing nervously at one another. They had no idea who these strangers were. But they sensed that they were warriors such as the Red Lancers only pretended to be.

The tall mouse curled his lip in contempt. 'Fun, you call it? I call it torture. You must be Captain Balbi. I've heard about you; a robber and a bully who serves that arch-robber and villain, Flambeau! Now, your mice are going to throw their weapons on the floor. If they don't, I'm going to cut your miserable throat.'

'No! Please. I – I meant no harm. Ow! Oh, Lord of Light, he means it! Drop your weapons, all of you!'

The stranger mouse sheathed his rapier as swords and pistols clattered to the floor. 'That's better. Now, is there a mouse here called Cranberry? Or Spital? Or Chowdmouse?'

Spital and Chowdmouse, who had been comforting their friend, looked up at the tall stranger. 'That's us.'

'I am honoured to meet the three loyal members of His Majesty's bodyguard. I am Lord Marengo, from the High Collada mountains, and these are my followers. Casey and his beavers are in the street outside. In a few hours, we shall have captured the Great Fortress and released the cardinal. Tell me: does this house have a cellar?'

'Yes, sir,' said Spital, pointing to a stout, oak door with heavy bolts.

'Nice and cool, is it?' asked Marengo with a grim smile.

Spital grinned. 'Flippin' freezin'!'

'Excellent! Captain Balbi, lead the way. You miserable mice, follow your wretched leader for the last time. Two of my warriors will remain on guard. If you behave yourselves, I may order your release in the morning. Any trouble, and you'll stay there for a month!'

The crestfallen Lancers trooped down to the cellar. When Marengo's mice had bolted the door, Chowdmouse whispered: 'Please, sir; like you said, we're the king's bodyguard. But where's the king?'

'I'm here.' A young mouse had entered the hall. Like Marengo's followers, he was dressed in colourful woollens. He was tall and powerfully built and as he drew near, the firelight shone on the reddish lights in his fur. His face wore a stern expression; but it broke into a warm smile as he recognised his friends. 'Cranberry! Spital! Chowdmouse! Oh, I'm so happy to see you again!'

For a moment, the three mice stared at Caladon. He seemed so much older than when they had last seen him. Then, they knelt before him. 'We ain't never forgotten you, yer Majesty,' whispered Chowdmouse.

'Things 'as been bad since you left,' said Spital. 'But now you're back, things is goin' to be all right, ain't they?'

Caladon raised his friends to their feet. 'Yes, Spital, I promise you! Lord Marengo, our mice are in position around the Great Fortress and I've sent Casey and the beavers along as reinforcements. I estimate about fifty Red Lancers on duty. There's no sign of my uncle, but no doubt he's skulking in there somewhere.'

Marengo bowed. 'Thank you, sir. Now, if your three bodyguards would care to arm themselves from the swords and pistols on the floor, I'm sure my followers can provide some warm coats for them. When we're ready, we'll go to the fortress and find your uncle. I fancy he's in for an unpleasant surprise!'

21 Eagles!

Aramon was in darkness. The duke had forbidden any mouse to leave his home, or even to light a candle, after the cathedral clock had tolled nine. Cranberry and his friends had been expecting Marengo to lead them to the Great Fortress, but, to their surprise, he led them in the opposite direction. 'Where we goin', Sir?' Spital asked Caladon.

'Through the West Gate. We overpowered the guards on our way in. Then, we're going to Barrowdown Moor.'

'Why?' asked Cranberry. 'I thought we were going to attack the fortress.'

'We are,' grinned Caladon. 'Wait and see . . .'

Beyond the West Gate, the mice followed the track across meadows and pastureland until the vast expanse of the moor lay before them. 'We came into the city to find you and the cardinal,' Caladon explained. 'Old Mother Bibo told us how poor Matthias had been arrested, and about how my uncle had stolen your new home; so we knew where to find you. We've left some mice and beavers hiding out near the Great Fortress in case my uncle discovers we're here and tries to make a run for it. But we're going in by a different way. Look!'

For a moment, the mice could see nothing but the dark curve of the moor beneath the twinkling stars. Suddenly, Spital gasped. 'Blimey! Are those eagles?'

Huge shadows were circling overhead. As the mice halted, the great eagles spiralled down and landed with a beating of wings. Cranberry was squeaking with excitement. He had heard so much about the famous Eagles of Carminel and had always longed to see them. Spital was gazing open-mouthed. Chowdmouse whispered: 'Are they goin' to attack the fortress?'

'We all are,' said Caladon with a smile.

'You mean – we're goin' on them eagles?'

'Of course. The one I ride is called Aquila. You three will come with me.'

'Brilliant!' exclaimed Cranberry.

'Yeah!' cried Spital.

'I'm scared of heights,' whispered Chowdmouse. 'But if I shut me eyes I'll be all right,' he added hastily.

'You won't be sick, will you?' asked Cranberry.

'I ain't had nuffink to eat since yesterday,' said Chowdmouse sadly, 'so I can't be!'

The thrill of his first eagle flight quickly banished Chowdmouse's fears. Sandwiched safely between Spital and Cranberry's comforting bulk, he snuggled among Aquila's warm feathers, staring in wonder at the great wings beating the air. Mounted on Hyperion, Aquila's father and a king among eagles, Marengo led the squadron in arrowhead formation towards the central tower of the Great Fortress.

The sentries were staring out over the city, unaware of their danger until a loud whooshing sound made them look up. For a moment they stared in frozen astonishment as a dozen eagles landed on the tower. As Marengo and his warriors sprang to the ground and drew their swords, the sentries yelled with fright, threw down their rifles, fled for the trapdoor and pelted down the steps into the fortress.

'After them!' The mice ran down the steps to the first landing. The long, torchlit passage stretched away in front of them. It was deserted, but from somewhere they could hear the sound of voices, raised in fear. 'Single file,' said Marengo. 'Follow me!'

The passage ended in a spiral staircase. Flaring torches, stuck in the wall, cast eerie shadows. Cranberry and Spital had drawn their borrowed pistols and looked as if they knew how to use them. But Chowdmouse had never touched one before. Spital had to show him which end to hold.

'And don't fiddle with it!' he hissed.

As they descended, the distant voices faded into silence. At the foot of the stairs, another passage stretched before them. At the far end stood Cardinal Matthias; but his paws were tied and Duke Flambeau's pistol was at his head. 'Go back!' cried the duke. 'Or the cardinal dies!'

'Don't listen to him,' said Matthias. 'My life is not important. Marengo, old friend, lead your warriors to victory over this tyrant!'

'Not at the price of your death, Matthias. We will go back.'

'Very sensible,' sneered Flambeau, lowering his

pistol slightly. 'Return to your mountains, you barbarians, and don't bother me again.'

Suddenly, a shot rang out. The bullet ricochetted off the ceiling, bringing down a cloud of dust, zinged off the floor, and flew up again, narrowly missing Flambeau's head. With a wild yell of terror, the Red Duke fled down the passage, yanked open a door and vanished.

'Who fired that shot?' demanded Marengo.

'It was me,' whispered Chowdmouse. 'I didn't mean to. It just sort of went off . . .'

'I told you not to fiddle with it!' exclaimed Spital. But Cardinal Matthias said: 'Don't be angry with him. Chowdmouse, surely the Lord of Light is with you tonight! I am unharmed, though I fear the duke has vanished. But we shall find him!'

'He went into my old bedroom,' said Caladon, putting his arm round the trembling Chowdmouse. 'There's a secret staircase leading to the postern gate. That's where he'll have gone.'

'Caladon,' said Marengo, 'take half the warriors to your room. If your uncle doubles back, grab him. Matthias, is there another way to the postern gate? If so, then please guide us there. Chowdmouse, come with us. I should be honoured to have such a doughty warrior under my command!'

But the postern gate, when they reached it, stood open; and though they searched the streets beyond, there was no sign of the duke. Marengo's warriors and the beavers who had been on watch outside had seen no one. 'We was watchin' the front door,' said Casey, 'while that varmint slipped out the back! Guess he might have headed for the water gate.'

'He'll be out of the city by now,' said Marengo. 'We'll send out an eagle patrol at dawn, though we'll be lucky to find him.'

The Red Lancers, terrified by the eagle warriors' attack, had taken refuge in the cellars. When they discovered that the duke had fled, they were only too glad to surrender. Marengo's mice rounded them up and herded them to the dungeons, releasing several city-mice imprisoned by Flambeau. These mice ran to Aramon and roused the city with the joyful news of Caladon's return.

Next morning, as the eagles took off in search of the duke, huge crowds gathered ouside the fortress, which was now flying the Royal Banner of Carminel. When Caladon appeared on the battlements, he was greeted with resounding cheers.

Accompanied by his three bodyguards, the king set off on a tour of the city. Crowds of mice followed him, rejoicing that the tyrant duke had fled. As they passed down Vittles Lane, Cranberry nudged Spital. 'There's my dad, up a ladder, painting out the 'Duke's Head'. The old tavern's getting its proper name back again.'

The Vittles Lane merchants pressed gifts on the king until he and his three friends were loaded with jewels, rare fruits, delicious pastries and fine robes. As they reached the harbour, a wonderful sight greeted their eyes. A proud ship was gliding in. Brightly-coloured flags fluttered from her yard-arms, and the Royal Banner of Carminel flew proudly at her masthead. As she dropped anchor, trumpets called from her quarterdeck and the captain's barge was lowered into the water.

A hush fell upon the crowd as Roamer stepped ashore and knelt before the king. 'We saw your flag flying from the fortress. Welcome home, your Majesty.'

Caladon grinned. 'And welcome home to you, Captain Roamer! What news do you bring?'

'Good news and bad, sir. The good news is that the Empress Ravanola is dead, we have the ruby and we rescued Princess Tamina.'

As the crowd yelled with delight, Caladon said: 'And the bad news?'

'Lukas is dead. Malatesta is on his way. We sighted

his fleet a week ago. With a fair wind, he will be here in a few days. We must prepare for war.'

22 The sword

That night, Caladon summoned the mice of Aramon to the Great Cathedral to witness the return of the ruby and to pray to the Lord of Light for help against Malatesta.

On the stroke of midnight, Cardinal Matthias unlocked the iron gates and mounted the steps to the high altar, where eleven tall candles were burning. He was carrying one of the treasures of Carminel: the Chalice of the Lord of Light. It was a plain, wooden bowl, found long ago by King Rufus the Great. After placing the chalice on the altar, the Cardinal stood in silent prayer, his eyes fixed on the great star that hung from the roof. After a while, he turned to the vast crowd of mice and cried: 'King Caladon, bring the ruby! Lord Marengo, bring the sword!'

Marengo and Caladon mounted the steps. Taking the softly-glowing ruby, Matthias placed it once again beneath the glass dome. Marengo drew his magnificent sword, which had once belonged to Gideon, the legendary eagle warrior, and hero of Carminel. His sword was now one of the treasures of Carminel and when Matthias placed it on the high altar, all three treasures, ruby, sword and chalice, were united.

'Great Lord of Light,' said the cardinal, 'Carminel is in peril greater than we have ever known. We ask your help in the struggle to come. Lord of Light, hear us!'

As with one voice, every mouse in the cathedral cried: 'Lord of Light, hear us!'

In the deep silence that followed, the ruby began to glow, brighter and brighter, until its scarlet light soared to the roof. At the same moment, silver light flowed from the chalice and multicoloured beams darted from the jewels on the sword's hilt until the light from the treasures mingled into one dazzling blaze.

And in the midst of the light appeared a great sword. Its blade gleamed like silver and a ruby shone from its hilt. As the mice gazed in wonder, silver light shone through the windows, bathing the mice in its gentle radiance. 'The Lord o' Light's star,' whispered Cheesemite, and Rio nodded slowly, 'Is miracle.'

Still the light poured from the treasures until the great sword was shining with an almost unbearable brilliance. As the cathedral became a dazzle of light, a voice spoke from out of the sword:

> *When the light is eclipsed and the darkness*
> *   is falling,*
> *Climb to the castle whose towers reach the sky.*
> *Seek for the sword in a garden of roses,*
> *Under the trees where the dead heroes lie.*
> *The humblest of mice shall discover the secret,*
> *Though treason may threaten, a young king*
> *   shall fight*
> *With the sword, and the Ruby of Power shall*
> *   defend him,*
> *And eagles shall lead you from darkness to light.*

The light faded, the sword vanished; the chalice and Marengo's sword ceased to shine. Only the ruby still glowed, its tiny heart beating strongly.

A great sigh arose from the mice. None doubted that they had seen a vision and heard the voice of the Lord of Light himself. Quietly, they rose to their feet, filed out of the cathedral and returned to their homes. At the Great Fortress, Caladon summoned his friends to a special council. Cranberry and Spital stood guard outside the door.

'Where is this castle?' asked Caladon. The mice shook their heads. No one knew.

There was a knock on the door and Chowdmouse entered, carrying a large, ancient book. He gave it to the cardinal. 'Is it the right one?' he whispered.

'Thank you, Chowdmouse, it is indeed. I sent him to my house for this,' said Matthias, as Chowdmouse joined his friends outside the door. 'It may give us the knowledge we need.' He blew a cloud of dust from the great book, and carefully turned the age-yellowed pages. 'Ah, yes, of course. I remember now. Listen to this:

> *It happened that in the reign of Vygan, first of the Mouse Kings, an army of rats, assisted by certain traitorous mice, fell upon the realm of Carminel.*

With fire and sword they ravaged the land, burning the fair city of Aramon to the ground and demanding the king's surrender. But King Vygan, scorning to yield to such barbarous foes, withdrew with his army to a great castle in the very heart of the kingdom. This castle was built upon a high rock, which so towered above the plain that mice called it the Castle in the Clouds.

Again and again, the rats tried to capture this mighty stronghold. But each time, they were driven back with grievous loss. For in truth, no enemy may take this castle, whose walls rise sheer from the precipice on which they stand and whose towers seem to pierce the sky. At last, seeing his enemies withering away, the king led out his mice against them. He drove them down to the plain, where, in a great battle, King Vygan utterly defeated the army of the rats, so that the few survivors were glad to slip away to their ships and return to their own land. Those traitorous mice who had assisted the enemy, hoping for gain, suffered the terrible death they so richly deserved.

But great was the sorrow among the mice, for in that battle King Vygan took his death wound.

Asked where he wished his body to lie buried, he said: 'Within the castle is a garden of roses. There will I lie. Take the ruby from my sword and give it to my son, for the Lord of Light himself gave it me, and it will defend the kings of Carminel from their enemies. But place my sword in the tomb with me. It must lie hidden, for there will come a time when a king of Carminel will have need of it. And so it was done.'

Matthias closed the book. For a while, no one spoke. At last, Princess Tamina broke the silence. 'The voice in the cathedral spoke of dead heroes. Who are they?'

'For a long time after the death of Vygan,' said the cardinal, 'heroes of Carminel were buried in the rose garden. Gideon himself lies there. The castle must have been a ruin for many years, though the walls and towers may still stand.'

'I see,' said Tamina. 'But the voice mentioned the "humblest of mice" – who can that be?'

'Who knows?' said Caladon. 'But the sooner we find this sword the better. Lord Marengo, six of your warriors should be enough for the task. Princess, how do you fancy a ride on an eagle?'

* * *

No one doubted that Malatesta's fleet would soon attack Aramon, and King Caladon worked hard to organise the city's defence. The Red Lancers were set free and were only too glad to swear loyalty to the king. They got their rifles back, and spent several hours being drilled by one of Marengo's mice, a fierce old warrior named Donal. 'Pick your feet up, you horrible little mice!' Donal would roar; 'Call yourselves soldiers? Faith an' begorrah, I've seen slugs an' snails that could march better! Squa-a-a-d, halt! That was terrible, so it was! Pre-sent arms! Too slow! Do it again! Ach, was ever a poor unfortunate captain landed with such a troop as this? But I'll lick you into shape, so I will!'

And he did. After two days, the Red Lancers were drilling and marching so smartly that Donal took them onto Barrowdown Moor for some serious training. Casey and his beavers helped by felling trees across the narrow streams to make bridges, which Donal would then teach the mice how to blow up. The crash of explosions echoed across the moor until the city mice thought that the stoats were upon them.

Twice a day, Marengo's eagles flew patrols, searching for Malatesta's ships. But they had not flown far when violent thunderstorms and torrential hail drove them back. 'At least the stoats won't be able to attack us in this weather,' said Marengo. 'And Malatesta may well lose some ships.'

But Roamer was worried. Tamina had told him of Gweir, whom she had heard about during her captivity. Roamer feared that the wizard was causing these storms, though why he should do so was more than Roamer could guess.

On the fifth evening after Tamina had flown off in search of the sword, Roamer was alone on the Great Fortress's high tower. Far below, Old Ben was organising groups of mice to strengthen the ancient walls; Rio was inspecting and repairing the worn timbers of the city's gates, while from distant Barrowdown, the thump of an explosion told of another bridge successfully blown up by Donal's Red Lancers.

Suddenly, eagles appeared, flying in from the north. They landed on the tower, and Roamer ran to greet the princess as she slid from Aquila's back. But his cheerful welcome died at the expression on her face.

'Prepare yourself for a shock, Roamer. Malatesta's outsmarted us. He landed his army on the west coast a week ago and marched inland, looting and burning farms and villages. By the time we arrived at the Castle in the Clouds, it was crawling with stoats. Malatesta's made it his headquarters and nothing short of a miracle will shift him. We're in big trouble!'

23 Caladon goes to war

In a small, cosy room, high in the Great Fortress, Tamina was toasting her toes at the fire. Between mouthfuls of mango, she told Roamer, Marengo and Matthias what she had seen at the Castle in the Clouds.

'How big is their army?' asked Marengo.

'Not as big as it would have been before Roamer blew up half their ships,' said Tamina. 'But I still couldn't count it. Well, sums never were my strong point. But they've loads more soldiers than we have.'

'What's the castle like?' asked Matthias.

'Oh, it's *enormous*. Perched on a hilltop, just like that old book said, only the hilltop covers a big area, so the castle really is huge. We flew over it several times. The stoats were running round in circles, thinking we were going to attack them. They sent up a squadron of vultures to attack us, but we simply climbed higher, until I almost had icicles drooping from my fur. Since vultures can't climb as high as eagles, they gave up.'

'Could you draw a plan of the castle?' asked Roamer.

'Certainly.' Matthias brought charcoal and paper and the others watched as the castle came to life under Tamina's skilful paw.

A long wall ran all the way round the hilltop; high, ruined towers stood at each corner. Other towers jutted out along the sides and a powerful gatehouse stood at one end. Just inside the gatehouse rose a tall, ruined keep and beyond that, Tamina sketched a variety of low buildings, barns, houses, even small fields. 'It's almost a town. Plenty of storage space for food, and there's a well just here, between gatehouse and the keep. Those fields are completely overgrown, of course; no one had been near the place for years before the stoats arrived. I'm afraid we couldn't tell where the garden of roses might be.'

'What's that?' asked Roamer. Tamina had drawn a

patch of shadow, just outside the wall, at the opposite end from the gatehouse.

'We were too high to be certain, but we thought it was a deep ravine. Apart from that, the walls simply rise straight from the hilltop, no ledge or anything, except here.' She put her paw in front of the gatehouse. 'A narrow track goes round the hill and ends in a wide space just there. But the stoats could easily fire down on it from the gatehouse, so that's not much help.'

'Are those trees?' asked Marengo, pointing to one side of the outer wall.

'Yes. Only two or three, growing out of the hillside, about as high as the wall. It's a bit ruined just there. Well, the whole place is a ruin, really. But it was so big and strong to begin with that being a ruin doesn't make much difference.'

'It is impossible to capture,' declared Matthias, shaking his head sadly.

'Difficult, certainly,' said Marengo.

'But not impossible,' said Roamer.

They all rose to their feet as Caladon came in. For a few moments he studied Tamina's drawing. 'The ravine on the north side is the key, of course. That and the gatehouse on the south side . . . and those trees could be useful.'

Roamer and Marengo stared at him in amazement. Caladon laughed. 'I spent my childhood working out ways of attacking pirate strongholds, pretending I was you, Roamer. I've spent all last winter in the mountains, hearing tales of Gideon, Rufus and I don't know how many other heroes. I ought to be able to see how a castle could be captured by now.'

'Well, it's more than I can see,' smiled the cardinal. 'But what about the poor country-mice who live nearby?'

'They're having a bad time,' said Tamina. 'We saw a gang of stoats leave the castle, run down the track and cross the plain to a farm. They just helped themselves to as much food as they could carry. Then they set fire to the place. On our way back, we saw several families of mice, all trudging towards Aramon. We landed and spoke to some of them. They said . . .'

'Go on,' said Caladon. 'What did they say?'

Tamina looked embarrassed. 'Well . . . they said what was the use of a king who couldn't protect them? They said they might as well have the Red Duke back again.'

Caladon stared in dismay. 'They're right,' he whispered.

'No, they're not!' cried Tamina. 'And we told 'em

181

so! I think the castle can be captured, and I'll get you that sword if it's the last thing I do!'

'Malatesta's been clever,' said Marengo. 'He knows that by raiding the countryside, he forces Caladon to march against him. By ancient custom, the king *must* defend his subjects. Malatesta's counting on us exhausting ourselves, trying to capture the castle.'

'Well, he's made a mistake,' said Roamer. 'Cheer up, Caladon! We'll get King Vygan's sword *and* take the castle!'

Next morning, crowds of cheering mice thronged the North Gate and lined the city walls as Caladon led his army off to war. Spital, Cranberry and Chowdmouse marched proudly with their king; next came Roamer and his buccaneers, followed by Casey and his beavers. Last in line marched Donal and his Red Lancers, who had changed their name to the Mouse Guards Blue, in honour of the blue and silver banner of Carminel. Many young city-mice had joined them, attracted by their smart appearance, and glad that the hated Captain Balbi was no longer with them; he was in prison in the Great Fortress, and was likely to remain there for some time.

A cheer went up as the Eagle Squadron soared into the sky. They circled the city to gain height, then took up an arrowhead formation behind Marengo and Hyperion, circling high above the army to guard against a surprise attack.

Old Matthias had wanted to come too, but Caladon had commanded him to stay behind and look after the city. Besides, the country-mice who were fleeing from Malatesta would soon be arriving and Matthias was the ideal mouse to organise food and shelter for them. He stood outside the gate, calling down a blessing on the soldiers as they marched away.

When the mice had vanished into the distance, old Matthias trudged slowly home to Mankinoles. Something was troubling him; something that the voice had said in the Great Cathedral: *Though treason may threaten* . . . Despite the warm sunshine, the old mouse shivered. Flambeau was still at large; and who else would threaten treason but the Red Duke?

24 Flash flood!

As Caladon's soldiers marched across fields and pastureland, they met sorrowful groups of country-mice whose homes the stoats had destroyed, trudging wearily towards the safety of Aramon. They stared blankly at the soldiers, wondering how so few could possibly defeat Malatesta's great army. Some of the younger mice, eager to hit back at the enemy, left their families and joined the Mouse Guards Blue. But most simply trekked on, stunned by what had happened to them.

On the sixth day, the army entered the Downlands.

They ran down steep-sided hills and splashed across shallow, gurgling streams until only one valley stood between them and a belt of forest; after that, they would see the Castle in the Clouds. But as Caladon crested the final ridge, he stopped abruptly and sent Spital hurrying back to fetch Roamer and Tamina.

Before them lay a deeper valley than any they had yet crossed. At first, the ground sloped gently. But far below, a fast-flowing river roared along its boulder-strewn bed between high walls of rock. The only way across was by a narrow rope bridge, secured at either end by a wooden post driven into the ground.

'I don't fancy our chances on that,' said Tamina. 'It looks as if a puff of wind would blow it away.'

'There are no trees on this side of the valley,' said Roamer. 'But on the far side of that ravine, there are plenty, some close to the edge.' Summoning Casey and the beavers, Roamer asked: 'Could you two cross that rope contraption and gnaw through a couple of trees on the far side? That would make a safer bridge.'

'No problem, Cap'n,' replied Casey.

'Wait,' said Caladon. 'I'll not ask you to do anything I'd not do myself. I'll come with you and cross the rope bridge first. Don't argue, Tamina. I'm going now.'

Followed by his bodyguards and the beavers, Caladon set off down the track. But no sooner had he gone, than Tamina gripped Roamer's paw in sudden alarm. A squadron of vultures, appearing out of nowhere, was streaking down the valley.

'Take cover!' yelled Roamer. The Mouse Guards Blue dodged behind trees or scurried under bushes. But the buccaneers unslung their rifles; they had faced vultures before and did not fear them. As the vultures dived for the ridge, Roamer yelled: '*Fire*!'

A volley crashed out. Through the choking smoke, the mice saw three vultures plummeting into the valley and the rest wheeling away, flying back the way they had come. The Mouse Guards Blue were cheering their heads off. But the buccaneers were swiftly reloading. They knew that the vultures would be back.

'Here they come again!' yelled Roamer. 'Don't fire till I give the word!'

The giant birds flew closer and closer. Sunlight gleamed on yellow talons and cruel beaks, and the mounted stoats were yelling and brandishing their swords.

Suddenly, out of the sun, came the eagles, diving on the vultures' right flank, and at that moment Roamer yelled: 'Fire!'

Caught between the buccaneers' close-range volley and the eagles' swift and sudden attack, the vultures broke and fled, the eagles streaking after them. The cheering mice waved and Marengo's riders grinned and waved back as the great eagles flew in pursuit of their beaten foe.

But one mouse was not cheering. 'What is it, Rio?' asked Roamer.

'I think you knows as well as I do, Capitano. Them vultures outnumbered the eagles by around two to one. Why they no stay an' fight, huh?'

'Because they're cowards,' said Tamina scornfully.

'In that case,' said Roamer, 'why did they fly west, down the valley, instead of north, towards their castle?'

'Oh! You mean they wanted the eagles to chase them? To draw them away? But why?'

'Maybe that's why!' Rio was pointing to the crest of the opposite slope. A lone vulture was perched on a branch. Beneath it, a stoat was raising his arms to the sky.

'He's holding a staff,' said Tamina. '*Gweir*!'

Behind the magician, dark clouds were building. As they rolled across the valley, Roamer knew what was going to happen. 'Rio! Get down to the bridge! *Tell Caladon not to cross*!'

But even as Rio hastened away, lightning stabbed the ravine, thunder roared and a dense curtain of rain blotted out the valley. The mice on the ridge ran for cover, but the rain slashed through the bushes, soaking the soldiers to the skin.

Rio was slipping and slithering down the slope, praying he would be in time. But when he reached the ravine's edge, he saw that Caladon was already halfway across the bridge. The beavers were watching anxiously, for the ropes were swaying in the rising wind.

'Hold on, sir!' yelled Casey. 'Hold on – oh, Lord of Light, *no*!'

With a loud crack, the end of the rope bridge nearest to them snapped from its mooring post. The sudden release of tension made Caladon lose his hold on the ropes. He felt himself falling, made a frantic grab for one of the dangling, swaying ropes, caught it and clung on, suspended over the raging torrent, feeling his grip weakening on the slippery rope.

Caladon looked down. White water tumbled and foamed, throwing up a drenching spray which seemed to pluck at his heels. He was drenched by the rain, dazzled by lightning, deafened by thunder. Suddenly, through his soaking clothes, he felt a warm glow. It was the ruby and he had completely forgotten about it.

He took one paw off the rope and dug frantically into his soaking pocket. At last, he grasped the ruby and pulled it free.

The beavers watching from the bank, and the mice up on the ridge, never forgot what happened next. An angry shaft of blood-red light shot from the ruby. Soaring above the ravine, it sprayed a dazzling fountain of light, multiplying its colours until a broad rainbow arched across the chasm. As the raindrops struck it, they rolled off, cascading onto the bank, while daggers of light pierced the clouds.

Gweir screamed in fury. He called upon the Snake-god and thunderbolts flew from his staff. But the Snake-god's power could not withstand the ruby. Gweir howled in agony as a rope of light twisted about his staff and wrenched it from his grip, sending it turning and tumbling into the ravine until the river swept it away.

The clouds rolled by, the rain stopped and warm sunshine flooded the valley. Slowly, the rainbow faded. Scarcely able to believe what had happened, Caladon slipped the ruby back in his pocket and clambered up the rope until he stood safely on the bank.

By the time Roamer had led the army down the slippery path, the water level had dropped. After its brief, destructive moments of freedom, the river was once more imprisoned between its high walls and the mice could hear its sullen roar as it rushed and tumbled far below.

Gweir shook his fists at the sky and cursed the Lord of Light. Then, he squelched to the tree where the vulture was perching. 'Get down from there! Take me back to the castle!'

But as Gweir scrambled aboard, some instinct made him glance up and he yelled in terror. The eagles had returned.

They were circling the valley, anxiously searching for any sign of the stoats advancing through the forest. As Gweir's vulture flapped out of the trees, Marengo caught sight of it. 'Hyperion! *Catch that vulture*!'

The great eagle swooped to treetop height. The vulture uttered a frenzied squawk and flew faster, but no vulture can out-fly an eagle and Hyperion was the swiftest of them all.

Gweir delved into his robes for his pistol. Twisting round, he waited until Hyperion was almost upon him, waited until he could see Marengo clearly. Then he squeezed the trigger. But the storm he had summoned had soaked his gunpowder and the pistol gave a harmless click. With a bitter curse, Gweir threw it away; then, he screamed as a shadow loomed over him and Hyperion's talons fastened around him. The great eagle plucked Gweir from the vulture's back and soared into the air until the valley below had dwindled into a ribbon.

Still gripping the helpless stoat, Hyperion streaked above the forest until the trees ended in a vast plain. From its centre, a high hill reared above the encircling grasslands. Spread out along the broad summit, its broken, jagged towers piercing the sky, stood the Castle in the Clouds.

Marengo could see tiny figures running to the walls, and he imagined the sudden panic Hyperion had caused. The eagle flew across the wall. High above the wide courtyard, he opened his talons. With a piercing shriek of mortal terror, Gweir, who had sought Caladon's life and cursed the Lord of Light, fell to his death.

Captain Blacktail hurried up the steps to the gatehouse roof where Malatesta was staring after the eagle. 'My lord! That was Gweir!'

'Serves him right,' muttered Malatesta. 'I ordered him to drown those mice at the ravine. Judging by those red lights in the sky which put an end to his feeble little storm, he obviously failed. Well, he's paid for it.'

'What shall we do, my lord?'

'Double the guard and send out some vultures. I want to know as soon as the first mouse pokes his snout out of that forest.'

'I meant about Gweir, my lord. Should we bury him? There's an old, disused graveyard just inside the north rampart. It's overgrown with brambles, but –'

'Fool! Why waste time on that good-for-nothing magician? Throw him over the wall!' Blacktail was shocked but he knew better than to argue with Malatesta.

As darkness fell, the vultures skimmed across the plain, their riders searching the forest. Stoats crowded the southem rampart, eager for their first glimpse of the mice. None felt scared. No army in the world could dislodge them from this castle. But there was no sign of Caladon's army.

Long after the vultures had returned and only the sentries watched the darkening plain, Malatesta stared from the gatehouse roof, brooding on the one mouse he truly hated. 'You've escaped me twice, Roamer,' he muttered. 'There won't be a third time, I swear it!'

25 The graveyard

Mounted on Hyperion, Marengo and Roamer were studying the castle. Stoats were yelling and brandishing their swords, but though they tried to shoot Hyperion down, the eagle scorned their feeble efforts, swooping repeatedly over the castle before soaring high above it. From such a height, the two mice could see the whole castle spread below them, like a model.

Outside the northern wall, a deep ravine cut like a wound into the steep hillside. Above the southern wall reared the great gatehouse. Within the encircling ramparts, the ruined keep's jagged towers looked like broken teeth. Beyond the keep, wide fields lay beneath a matted tangle of weeds with here and there a ruined barn or outbuilding. But there was no sign of the rose garden where lay King Vygan's tomb.

'No fires,' ordered Caladon that evening, 'lest the rising smoke betray our position to the stoats.'

The mice gnawed uncooked food, by now grown hard and stale. 'This bread's like rock,' groaned Spital, 'and my cheese has gone all mouldy.'

'Real soldiers' food!' grinned Cranberry. 'Donal of the Mouse Guards Blue says that once this has run out, we'll get no more until we win it with our swords!'

'I hope he'll win some for me,' whispered Chowdmouse. ' 'cos I ain't a real soldier!'

'Listen, you two,' said Spital quietly. 'I've 'ad an idea. Marengo an' Roamer can't find this 'ere magic sword, 'cos they can't find the rose garden. But we can!'

'How?' asked Cranberry eagerly.

'Simple. We cross the plain, then head for the other side of the castle, right? There's thick cloud tonight, so the stoats won't see us. Then we climb the hill, nip up them trees, over the wall, and find the graveyard.'

'Yeah!' Cranberry's eyes were shining. 'You up for it, Chowdmouse?'

Chowdmouse was horrified. They could never hope to climb that hill! But he could not bear to be left behind. 'We'd best wear our cloaks,' he whispered. 'They'll help to hide us.'

The three adventurers walked boldly out of the camp. The sentries, thinking that they were acting on Caladon's orders, did not stop them. They were glad of their cloaks, for halfway across the plain, a cold drizzle began to fall. By the time they had crept round to the far side of the hill, the mice were soaked and shivering.

'The climb'll warm us up,' said Spital, through chattering teeth.

'We'll never climb that!' Cranberry was staring in dismay at the almost sheer cliff, so high that the castle was invisible.

'We can't turn back now,' sighed Chowdmouse. 'Let's 'ave a go . . .'

They set off, groping for paw-holds and hauling themselves up the slippery rock, helped by occasional tufts of grass. By the time they were halfway up, the rain was falling heavily, driven by a cold wind that whistled across the hillside. But with many a backward slip, they clambered on. Spital led the way, taking his time, directing and encouraging the others. Cranberry, whose bulk made climbing difficult, was panting hard. Chowdmouse, who hated heights, was trying not to look down. But when he looked up, he saw the stoats patrolling the black line of ramparts, so he stared at the grass and rock in front of him, wishing he was back home in Aramon.

At last, wet through and trembling with exhaustion, Spital grasped the twisted tree roots that marked the summit. Hauling himself to a narrow ledge, he reached down and helped the others until at last, they all collapsed in the shadow of the wall. The rain had stopped, but it still felt bitterly cold. Trying to calm their panting breath, they listened, for they could no longer see the sentries. But no sound broke the silence save the sighing of the wind.

'Come on,' whispered Spital. 'We can't stop 'ere all night. Got to climb this tree. I'll go first.'

Though the branches gave plenty of footholds, Spital felt horribly exposed, for the bare twigs gave no cover. When he was level with the top of the wall, he crouched along a branch and peered left and right. Only one stoat was in sight, marching slowly away towards the distant keep. Spital hissed: 'All clear!'

Once over the battlements, the mice hurried along the slippery stone ledge. The way was so narrow and the ground so far below, that Chowdmouse felt his stomach churning. He kept his eyes on his feet and followed closely behind the others until at last they came to a flight of steps and were able to leave the wall.

'Which way?' whispered Cranberry. Far off to their right, loomed the tall ruined keep. Several smaller buildings crouched in its shadow. But in the other direction, the fields of weeds offered cover as far as the north rampart, where a large area of wasteground lay like a dark smudge. 'That way,' whispered Spital.

The wind was sweeping across the hilltop, and the dark clouds, low in the sky, were scudding before it. 'The stars'll be out soon,' hissed Cranberry. 'But the wind's keeping these weeds moving, so the stoats won't see us . . . I hope!'

At last, the field ended and a long, low barrier barred their way. So overgrown was it with moss and trailing weeds that it was a while before the mice realised it was a stone wall. Keeping low to the ground, they followed it until they reached a tall arch. Beyond, lay a dark, tangled wilderness of long, twisting stems, so thick they were more like branches, covered in long, wicked spikes.

'Brambles,' hissed Spital.

'Roses,' whispered Chowdmouse.

The clouds parted and moonlight bathed the ancient wall in silver. Cranberry gasped and pointed to the top of the arch. Carved in the stone was the Star of the Lord of Light. 'You're right, Chowdy,' whispered Spital. 'I think we've found it. Come on!'

As the three mice were creeping beneath the arch, Scratchfur, Piebald and a platoon of Ermine Guards were following Captain Blacktail out of the ruined keep. Blacktail was feeling extremely nervous; he had disobeyed Malatesta's orders.

Although he had never liked Gweir, Blacktail could not bring himself to throw the wizard's body over the ramparts. No stoat deserved that. Telling his soldiers that Malatesta had ordered him to bury Gweir during his off-duty hours, Blacktail ordered them to gather up the body and to follow him to the ancient graveyard.

Armed with pickaxes and spades, they tramped across the fields to the stone arch and were about to enter the graveyard, when Blacktail suddenly caught an alien smell . . . 'Mice!'

'But it can't be, sir,' said Scratchfur. 'They couldn't

have climbed the hill! Besides, what would mice be doin' in this 'ere boneyard?'

'Spying, probably! Stay here. If they come out, grab them. I'm going in.'

Deep inside the graveyard, the mice were creeping beneath the arching tangle of roses. No buds grew along those twisted stems; only the cruel thorns gleamed in the moonlight. Suddenly, above the pounding of his heart, Chowdmouse heard a rustling in the grass behind him.

'Wait!' he hissed. 'Listen!'

They stopped. Silence. Even the wind had died. 'You're imagining things,' said Cranberry. 'Lead on, Spits!'

But Chowdmouse hesitated, certain he had heard something. He strained his eyes, searching back the way they had come. When at last he turned to follow the others, they had vanished.

Chowdmouse was close to panic. Desperate to find his friends, he went deeper and deeper into the graveyard. Suddenly, he stopped, his heart racing. Looming above him through the tangle of rose stems, was a giant bird, its wings outspread, its dark eyes staring straight at him. Stifling a cry of terror, Chowdmouse was about to turn and run, when he realised that the bird was made of stone.

Greatly wondering, Chowdmouse crept towards it. A stone mouse, wearing a cloak and brandishing a sword, sat astride the great bird and it dawned on Chowdmouse that the bird was an eagle. *And the mouse must be Gideon*, he thought. *I've heard of him. But I never thought I'd see his tomb!* He ducked beneath the great wings and found himself on a grassy pathway. Tall trees pierced the tangle of rose stems and at the far end a stone tomb glimmered in the moonlight.

As Chowdmouse crept along the path, he saw other statues: mice, with upraised swords, as if turned to stone in the act of leading a charge for freedom. *This is the place*, he thought; *this is where the heroes of Carminel are buried*. Reaching the tomb, Chowdmouse saw lines of writing, carved into the flat surface. As he stared at them, a silver beam lanced down from the sky, turning the writing to flickering lines of fire. The great Star of the Lord of Light was shining directly above him and a voice in his head said: 'Read!'

But the burning lines of light meant nothing. Chowdmouse humbly bowed his head. 'I can't read.'

'Then listen carefully,' said the kindly voice, 'and remember . . .

200

Beneath this stone the bones of Vygan lie,
A king, mighty in war, who also gave
His realm good laws and many a year of peace.
At last, he fell, most piteously slain.
But when the land lies bleeding unto death,
And Carminel seems lost, mark well these words:
This stone is sealed, none may raise the lid;
But One shall find the sword that here lies hid.

Chowdmouse gazed in wonder at the star. 'I'll remember,' he whispered. As the light faded, he looked again at the tomb. Beneath the writing, darker than the darkness, lay the carved image of a great sword.

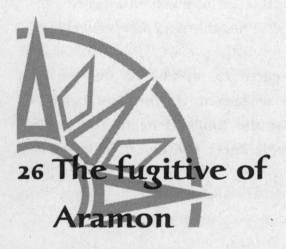

26 The fugitive of Aramon

Chowdmouse ran his paws over the carved sword. Where the blade met the hilt, a circular hole seemed to be waiting for the great ruby.

Quivering with excitement, Chowdmouse hurried down the path. As he slipped beneath the carved eagle, the roses raised their stems to let him pass, guiding him back towards the arch. At last, he reached it and saw shadowy figures waiting for him. But as he ran towards them, he stopped abruptly. His friends were prisoners of the stoats.

'Run fer it, Chowdy!' cried Spital. But Piebald and Scratchfur were moving to cut him off. He darted back towards the arch, hoping to lose his pursuers among the tangled roses. But even as the archway loomed above him, he stopped and slumped in defeat. Another stoat had emerged from the grave-yard, his pistol pointing at Chowdmouse's heart.

'Got you!' said Captain Blacktail. 'I heard you crashing about in there. All I had to do was wait. How you three got into the castle I can't imagine. But your little spying expedition's over. Malatesta will be very interested to see you.'

The Ermine Guards dragged them across the field. The mice felt terribly afraid. They could expect no mercy from Malatesta. 'Did you bury that wizard?' Blacktail asked Piebald.

'Aye, sir, beside the wall, while we was waitin' fer these mice. Ground were nice and soft.'

'Good. I daresay you'll have three more graves to dig before long.'

The mice felt sick. The stoats laughed. Suddenly, they cried out in alarm, shielding their eyes as dazzling light flooded over them. 'It's only a star!' yelled Blacktail. 'Keep going! And hang on to those mice!'

But Scratchfur was yelling a warning; two

shadows were rippling across the grass. The mice were hurled to the ground as the stoats flung themselves flat. Two eagles landed behind them in a flurry of wings and their riders swiftly dismounted.

'Run for the keep!' yelled Blacktail. But as they ran, dragging the mice behind them, their way was blocked by another eagle with outstretched wings and gaping beak. As Marengo slid to the ground, the stoats gave a wild cry, abandoned their prisoners and fled. Blacktail drew his pistol; but he was outnumbered and knew he would be killed if he tried to fight the Eagle Warriors. With a bitter curse, he took to his heels and followed his fleeing soldiers.

'These stoats are cowards,' remarked Marengo. 'I was looking forward to a fight! Well, you three, thank the Lord of Light we found you, for it was his star that showed us where you were. Climb aboard! King Caladon's furious with you, so I hope you've a good excuse for what you've done tonight!'

The eagles landed on the edge of the forest and the warriors escorted the three mice through the trees. Caladon was waiting. His brows were drawn in a scowl and his voice was stern indeed. 'Well? What have you been up to?'

'We went to find ol' Vygan's tomb,' muttered Spital.

'You're crazy!' cried Caladon.

'Did you climb the hill and get into the castle?' asked Roamer.

'Yes,' said Cranberry. 'And we found the graveyard.'

'Did you find the tomb?' asked Tamina.

'No,' groaned Spital.

'Yes,' whispered Chowdmouse.

'You risked your lives and those of the Eagle Warriors,' said Caladon sternly. 'Your punishment . . . *Chowdmouse! What did you say?*'

Meanwhile, the mice of Aramon were waiting anxiously for news. Every day, they lined the city walls, scanning the horizon for any sign of a messenger and searching the sky, lest Marengo should send an Eagle Warrior with news of a victory or the tragic tidings of defeat.

Cardinal Matthias laboured daily to find food and lodging for the country-mice who were pouring into the city and spreading dreadful tales of the savage stoats. Though by evening Matthias was exhausted, he always went to the Great Cathedral to pray for victory; and it was during these times, whilst he knelt before the candlelit altar, that he became aware that he was not alone.

At first, the sound was so faint that he thought he was imagining it: a gentle rustling, seeming to come from the high rafters, invisible in the gloom. One night, he thought he heard creaking, as if a door were being cautiously opened. Hardly an evening passed without his hearing some faint sound; but though he took a candle and searched the cathedral, he found nothing.

Matthias was old and stairs tired him. Had he been younger, he might have ventured up the worn steps that led to the bell tower. At one point, about three quarters of the way up, these steps opened out to form a landing. A low door led to a narrow platform; beyond, a long wooden beam stretched the whole length of the building. From the beam, huge rib-like rafters soared to the roof; and among these Matthias would have found the source of the strange, soft sounds.

A mouse was living there, a hunted creature, who had slunk back one dark night into the city that had cast him out. Sneaking into the cathedral, he had climbed the steps, opened the door and crawled out onto the beam. From there, he had clambered high into the rafters and where several were grouped together, like branches spreading from the trunk of a tree, he had made his home.

Every night, he crept into the city, scavenging through rubbish bins for scraps to eat. Hiding them beneath his cloak, he would scuttle back through the dark streets, clamber to his perch and chew the rotting food. Though he had grown skilful at moving quietly, the door creaked and the old beams and rafters occasionally betrayed his presence. It was these faint sounds that Matthias heard.

Insects, the cardinal decided; woodworm or perhaps the deathwatch beetle. Had he known the truth, he would have been horrified. For the fugitive who crouched among the rafters, his heart eaten up with hatred and counting the days until he should take revenge upon his enemies, was none other than Flambeau, Red Duke of Aramon!

27 The Sword of Vygan

This stone is sealed, none may raise the lid
But One may find the sword that here lies hid.

'I dunno how you'll raise the lid, sir,' said Chowdmouse thoughtfully. 'But you must be the one to find the sword. Anyway, that's what the writin' said. A voice come from the star an' told me to remember. So I did.'

'You're a marvel!' cried Caladon.

'You're a remarkably brave and intelligent young mouse,' said Marengo warmly. 'I wish you were in my Eagle Squadron.'

Chowdmouse ducked his head. Such praise had never come his way before. 'Thanks. But I'm scared of heights.'

'He's my bodyguard,' said Caladon, 'and I wouldn't change him for all the eagles of Carminel! Well, now that we know where the sword's to be found, we march tonight!'

All that day, the mice forgot their gnawing hunger and sharpened their swords, cleaned their firearms and boasted of the brave deeds they would perform when they came to grips with the stoats! But as the last gleams of sunlight faded from the forest and darkness cloaked the plain, many mice felt fear creeping over them. Caladon sensed the changed atmosphere and called them all together.

'The waiting is over! Tonight, we march against the strongest enemy Carminel has ever faced. We are few, they are many – though not as many as they would have been, thanks to Captain Roamer and his brave buccaneers!' The mice raised a cheer. Caladon felt their terror drawing back and courage surging forward. 'I know you will fight bravely. Those who fall, and go to the Lord of Light on his Island of Peace, will never be forgotten. Those who live, can tell their children with pride of what they did tonight! Now we must go. We shall meet again at the victory feast! You know your places; may the Lord of Light be with you all!'

They cheered him and trooped away, grinning at each other in the darkness. As they left the camp, they split into two groups. Donal and the Mouse Guards Blue swung left, following the trees until, across the plain, they saw the castle gatehouse outlined against the sky. Its battlements were in darkness, though the gleam of lanterns along the western wall showed where the stoats were watching the track.

But Donal's mice were not heading for the track. They were making for the southern slope that ended in the open space before the gatehouse. It was a much steeper climb. But the stoats would not expect them to come that way. Spreading out, they crept across the fields to the foot of the hill. Now they could relax; from the height of the gatehouse, they were invisible.

'From three ranks,' Donal called softly. 'All weapons muffled? When I give the word, climb silently as you value yer lives! If I hear so much as a whisper from anyone, I'll put a bullet in him, so I will!' The mice grinned, Donal raised his paw and they began to climb.

Meanwhile, Roamer and Tamina were leading the

buccaneers and the beavers in the opposite direction, towards the northern ramparts and the deep ravine. Caladon was with them, escorted by his bodyguards. 'Easier climb for us tonight,' grinned Cranberry.

'Oh, yeah?' Spital's face was grim. 'What about that ravine, then? Climbin' down that *an' up again* won't be a picnic. The bottom's a mass of boulders. One wrong step an' yer done for.'

'That's why the beavers are here,' whispered Chowdmouse. 'They're goin' to gnaw through that tree on this side of the ravine to make a bridge.'

'Who told you that?' asked Spital.

'Nobody. I worked it out for meself. It's true, ain't it, sir?'

'Yes, and once over the wall, we're depending on you to guide us to the tomb.'

Chowdmouse had been afraid of that. He doubted he could find the tomb again. But he put on a brave face. 'I won't let yer down.'

Between sunset and moonrise, the eagles rose from the plain. Soaring high, they slowly circled the castle, awaiting the moment to attack. Years of training above the mountains now paid off, for the warriors scarcely felt the bitter cold and the eagles could stay aloft for hours on end.

Donal's mice were struggling up the hill, forcing

their weary limbs from one narrow ledge to the next. Though Donal was one of Marengo's toughest warriors, he was feeling the strain, for attached to his back by a rope cradle was a small but weighty powder barrel. At last, just below the summit, they reached a grassy ledge that ran round the hillside. Gasping and panting, they flung themselves down. 'Get this barrel off me,' whispered Donal. 'We'll wait here till it's time . . .'

On the northern slope, the tree's dark outline was drawing closer as Roamer and the buccaneers clambered towards the northern ramparts. Cheesemite, who was used to scampering up the *Avenger*'s rigging in a raging storm, found the climb easy. But Rio was wheezing and gasping by the time they crested the ridge. He leaned gratefully against the tree, trying to ignore the dark ravine that yawned below.

'Shift yourself, Rio,' said Roamer. 'The beavers have work to do.'

'No rest for Rio!' muttered the carpenter. But he made way for Casey's beavers, who attacked the tree with their razor-sharp teeth. The crash as it fell sounded horribly loud, but the wall beyond was unguarded and far from the keep. Leaping onto the fallen tree, Caladon led the buccaneers across, trying not to look down at the dark ravine. When all had safely crossed and were crouching below the wall, Old Ben unwound his rope and flung the noose. It caught round the broken battlements and Roamer swiftly clambered up.

Below the wall, a sea of rose-stems rose and fell. The distant keep was in darkness, though lights along the western wall showed where the stoats still watched the path.

Tamina swung herself over the wall and stared at the graveyard. 'Goodness, what a maze! Let's hope Chowdmouse remembers the way . . .'

Chowdmouse led the buccaneers beneath the thorns, where the waning moonlight hardly penetrated. He could not see the trees that marked the tomb. *I'm lost*, he thought miserably, *the attack will fail and it will be all my fault!*

'Not long till dawn,' whispered Tamina. 'Are you sure we're going the right way, Chowdy?'

'No,' husked Chowdmouse. 'I don't know where we are . . .'

'Well, I do! Look over there, where the rose stems are lifting! They're showing the way!' Relief flooding through him, Chowdmouse hurried along the thorny tunnel. As the mice passed the stone eagle, it seemed that Gideon was pointing the way to Vygan's tomb.

'Here it is! There's the writin' and you can just make out the shape of the sword.'

'But how do we get it?' asked Tamina. 'The writing says the tomb is sealed.'

'Let's try and lift the lid,' said Roamer. They heaved and strained, but not even Rio could move the solid stone. While the buccaneers wrestled with the lid, the moonlight faded, leaving them in utter darkness.

From the ridge below the gatehouse, the Mouse Guards Blue watched as moonlight drained from the sky. 'Get ready, lads!' hissed Donal. 'Any second . . . *now*!' Leaping to his feet, he scrambled up the last of the slope, two mice following with the powder barrel. Knowing that the stoats must see them soon, they stumbled over the stretch of open ground and had almost reached the gatehouse when a cry from the battlements pierced the darkness and the walls erupted in smoke and flame and a hail of bullets poured down.

Roamer heard the distant gunfire. The attack had started! 'Think! There must be a way to get the sword! What does the writing say?'

'One shall find the sword,' said Tamina. 'That must mean Caladon . . . Of course! The ruby!'

Caladon took it from his pocket. The ruby's fierce

glow banished the darkness and was so hot that Caladon yelped and dropped it onto the tomb. It rolled along the deep, carved sword, coming to rest on the cross-piece of the hilt.

Red light exploded, the lid split open with a rending crash and the ruby fell into the tomb. Caladon caught a brief glimpse of a pile of dust. Beside it lay an ancient, crooked sword. There was a hole in the hilt, just as there had been on the carved image. As the ruby dropped into place, the mice gasped and hid their eyes from the searing white light that blazed from the tomb.

But Caladon forced himself to look. In that white heat, the sword was being forged anew. Golden thread glittered on the handle, the blade gleamed silver and the ruby poured out wave after wave of light.

Gradually, the heat grew less intense. Caladon leaned in and grasped the sword. As he raised it above his head, light shot from the blade and soared into the sky where it mingled with the silver beams pouring from the Lord of Light's great star.

'The sword is ours!' cried Caladon. 'Follow me!' Tangled stems barred their way; but, as Caladon hacked them down, starlit roses bloomed among the thorns.

With every stem that Caladon cut through, more roses bloomed until the air was heavy with their scent. At last, the arch loomed above them. The firing sounded louder and they hurried across the fields towards it.

Tamina paused and looked back. The whole graveyard was a mass of roses. 'Oh, how beautiful,' she whispered. Then she drew her sword and ran after the others towards the sound of the guns.

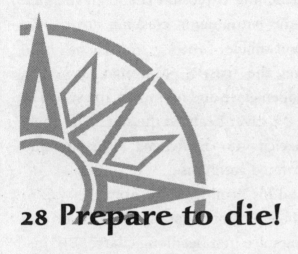

28 Prepare to die!

'Sure, an' it's not so very different from blowin' up a bridge,' grinned Donal. He and his mice were crouching against the castle gate. Directly above them, where the battlements jutted out, the stoats were firing blindly into the darkness. But the mice were invisible to their enemies.

'Put the barrel hard against the gate,' said Donal. 'Now put in the fuse, just like I've taught you. Good! Now pass the tinder-box.' He struck a flame and the fuse crackled into life. From below the hill's crest, the Mouse Guards Blue saw the fizzing firework and at once fired a murderous volley at the battlements.

The stoats yelled and ducked. Donal and his mice pelted away, tumbling over the ridge to join their friends as a deafening explosion shattered the gate and brought the battlements crashing down in a smoking heap of rubble.

High above the castle, Marengo saw the explosion's sudden glare and his sword, the sword of Gideon, flashed a silver beam to the stars. The Eagle Squadron wheeled into arrowhead formation and dived for the ruined gatehouse.

Malatesta and his Ermines leapt from the wall to the pile of rubble as Donal sprang from cover and led his cheering mice in a headlong charge. But just as Malatesta yelled 'Fire!' his stoats saw Marengo's gleaming sword and the great eagles swept overhead, sending the enemy reeling.

'Stand and fight, you cowards!' screamed Malatesta, but already Donal's mice were streaming up the fallen gatehouse and the eagles were circling for another charge. With a furious curse, Malatesta fired his pistols at the advancing mice; then he ran back, yelling at his Ermines to take shelter in the keep.

Out in the fields, Captain Blacktail and his riders

were waiting with the vultures. Seeing Malatesta's Ermine Guards in headlong flight, Blacktail scrambled aboard his vulture and the squadron soared into the sky. But Marengo saw the danger. He raised his sword, the eagles turned into the charge and smashed into the vultures. High above the castle, the two lines locked and swayed, pistols flashing, beaks and talons tearing; then the eagles broke clear and Marengo led them in a soaring climb, the vultures streaking after them.

'We've beaten them!' screeched Blacktail. 'Let's finish 'em off!'

Suddenly, Marengo's sword flashed in the darkness. The eagles turned and swooped upon their prey. As the battlelines clashed again, pistols snapped, swords flickered and flashed, beaks and talons ripped and clawed. Suddenly, through that hellish confusion, Marengo spotted Blacktail. As Hyperion streaked past, Marengo swung his sword in a mighty cut and Blacktail, with a terrible cry, toppled and fell.

Seeing their leader fall, the rest of the vultures wheeled and fled, racing for the safety of the forest. Marengo raised his sword again, a beam of light lanced into the sky and another band of eagles, who had been circling the battle, swooped upon the fleeing enemy, hunting them down until not one vulture remained alive.

Marengo's eagles swooped again, this time on the sentries lining the western wall who were firing down on the Mouse Guards Blue. Yelling in terror, the stoats fled from the ramparts, running to join the Ermine Guards who were streaming towards the keep. But now, out of the darkness, came Caladon and the Sword of Vygan.

Brandishing the mighty sword, the king carved his way through the stoats, Roamer, Tamina, and the sea-mice hard at his heels. Rio was swinging his cutlass, roaring at the stoats and keeping an eye on Cheesemite, who was taking care to stick close to his powerful shipmate. Tamina, her golden fur blackened with powder-smoke, fired into the darkness, seeing with fierce delight the enemies of her tribe reel and fall.

Roamer was keeping close to Caladon, fearing lest the young king, fighting his first battle, should run himself headlong into danger. But Caladon might have been born for this moment. His shouts of praise and encouragement rose above the battle, and his mice cheered him again and again. Light streamed from his great sword, no stoat could stand against it, and Caladon wielded it with such strength that his path was littered with dead and wounded until the enemy could take no more. With a cry of despair, they turned and fled. But there was no escape, for they crashed straight into Donal's mice, charging up from the gatehouse. Trapped between two enemies, the stoats flung down their weapons and cried for mercy.

But the battle was not over yet. As Donal's mice rounded up the prisoners, gunfire crashed from the ruined keep. 'Malatesta's in there!' cried Caladon. He raised his sword, his eyes sweeping across his army, willing them to one last effort. Cranberry, Spital and Chowdmouse were quivering with exhaustion, but from their steadfast eyes Caladon knew they would not fail him. The others, too, were weary, many were limping from wounds. But their king had proved himself a leader. They would not let him down.

'What are we waiting for?' yelled Tamina.

Caladon laughed. 'Form ranks! Are you ready? Charge!'

With a wild yell, the buccaneers and the Mouse Guards Blue dashed for the keep. Leaping for a yawning gap in the ruined walls, they scrambled over, and Malatesta's Ermines fell back before their furious attack. Caladon's sword was a beacon of victory and the mice swept after it.

'Hold them! Hold them!' Malatesta's scream rose above the roar of battle. But his Ermines were retreating. Piebald and Scratchfur turned to run, but both fell victim to Rio's mighty cutlass. 'Any more of you stinkin' stoats feel like a fight?' yelled the carpenter, glaring round furiously. Few did. Many were flinging down their weapons and begging for mercy. Roamer was searching for Malatesta. But the Ermine Lord was nowhere to be seen.

Tamina was leaning on her sword, gasping for breath, when a sudden movement caught her eye. In the far corner of the keep, a stoat was scuttling for the spiral staircase. Tamina saw the spike on his paw; but without a second thought, she dashed across and climbed after him.

As she ran up the steps, the cheers of the victors and the cries of the wounded faded into silence. Tamina paused, trying to calm her panting breath. Footsteps echoed faintly from above. Leaving her sword, she drew her pistol and padded silently upwards.

At the top of the steps, Tamina found herself on a wide, windswept platform, encircled by crumbling battlements. She took a step forward. The tower seemed deserted. Suddenly, she heard a footstep behind her and she leapt aside as the spike came flashing down.

Malatesta was backing her towards the battlements. His spike was raised again and a sword gleamed in his other paw. Tamina pointed her pistol. 'Surrender, stoat! Your army's beaten. You're finished!'

Shadows were snaking round Malatesta's heels. His eyes were cold and cruel. 'You can't kill me. I am under the Snake-god's protection. You've meddled with me once too often, tamarin. Prepare to die.'

Tamina pulled the trigger. The hammer fell, flint and steel flashed. But no bullet flew from the barrel. With a thrill of horror, Tamina realised she had forgotten to reload it.

'A flash in the pan, dear Princess,' sneered Malatesta. His sword swept down, Tamina leaped sideways and the sword crashed against the battlements, sending a shower of broken stones crashing to the ground. Malatesta turned with a snarl, Tamina hurled the pistol in his face, but he ducked and sword and spike flashed down together.

Tamina sprang clear, backing swiftly away from the edge. As Malatesta whipped round after her, she stumbled and fell. Curling herself up, she grasped her ankles, her eyes pleading for mercy. Malatesta laughed and raised his spike for the kill. He was still laughing when Tamina drew the dagger from her boot and hurled it with all her strength. Malatesta screamed, staggered back and crashed against the battlements. The ancient stones gave way and, with a howl of mortal terror, the Ermine lord vanished over the edge.

29 Duel to the death

The victory had been dearly bought. Many mice lay dead or wounded. Donal had been cut down by Malatesta; several beavers would never see their mountains again. The sorrowing soldiers gently carried their fallen comrades to the graveyard. They buried them among the ancient heroes of Carminel and the roses shed their petals over them, like tears.

Tamina was quivering with shock after her narrow escape. But seeing the wounded mice lying helpless on the battlefield, she pushed aside the thought of Malatesta and the glittering spike that had so nearly ended her life. Rolling up her sleeves, she set to work with her splints and bandages. For an hour or more she laboured, talking cheerfully to the wounded. Rio, Cheesemite and other buccaneers helped. But it was the golden princess the injured mice wanted in their pain; and in helping them she soon forgot that terrible moment on the castle rooftop when only her little dagger had stood between her and death.

Knowing that Caladon wanted a victory feast, Roamer was searching for food. He explored the ruined keep until he found the door to the cellar, which, as he soon discovered, was where the stoats had been hoarding their plundered stores.

'It's stuffed with potatoes, cabbages, mushrooms, apples, nuts and cheese,' he told Caladon; 'flagons of good country cider, too. It all belongs to the local farmers but they'll not begrudge it and there's enough treasure aboard the *Avenger* to pay for it!'

When the wounded mice had been made as comfortable as possible, Tamina joined her friends round the fire and tucked in to a bowl of mushrooms smothered in melted cheese. Everyone had heard how she had slain Malatesta; Caladon and Roamer were loud in their praise. But she frowned and shook her head.

'I'd rather not think about it, if you don't mind. I've never been so scared in my life!'

Marengo tactfully changed the subject. 'What will you do with the sword, Caladon?'

'Keep it! It is the greatest treasure of Carminel . . . Oh, Lord of Light, *look*!'

Something was happening to the sword. The golden thread on the hilt was shrivelling away and the shining blade was turning dark and rusty, its keen edge blunt and twisted, just as it had looked when Caladon first saw it.

The others cried out in disappointment. But Caladon understood. 'The sword has done its work. It's helped us to victory. Now we must replace it in the tomb. Who knows? One day, another Mouse King may need it . . .'

Leaving the army to their feast, Caladon led Tamina, Roamer and Marengo across the fields to the graveyard. The roses lifted their heads in greeting and the air was sweet with their scent. When the companions reached the broken tomb, Caladon laid the old sword to rest. Taking the ruby, he held it high and with a deep rumble, the broken halves of the lid glided together until it was impossible to see where the split had been. Greatly wondering, the friends turned to leave; as they passed beneath the tangled stems, rose petals softly fell, making a red carpet for the victorious king.

When the army was ready to return to Aramon, Caladon summoned Marengo. 'Let the Eagle Squadron fly to the city with news of our victory. Tell them that Malatesta is dead, valiantly slain by the princess, and that Carminel is free! Take the ruby; bid Cardinal Matthias replace it in the Great Cathedral for all our mice to see.'

The army cheered as the eagles soared into the air. But Roamer said: 'You shouldn't have done that. The ruby exists to protect you.'

'But Malatesta is dead, and some of the Mouse Guards Blue are taking the prisoners to their ships. Who's left to fear?'

'Flambeau – the Red Duke.'

Caladon laughed. 'My uncle? He's probably fled the country by now! Don't look so serious, Roamer! It's over. Let's go home. Nothing can harm us now!'

The mice marched home in triumph. As they drew near to Aramon, the country-mice who had sought shelter in the city flocked to greet them. Marengo had spread the joyful news and as the soldiers crested the last hill and saw Aramon glowing in the sunshine, the pealing of bells came floating to their ears.

The Eagle Squadron was circling the city, the walls were lined with cheering mice. Old Matthias, waiting at the North Gate, ran to embrace Caladon and cried a blessing on the returning warriors. As the buccaneers marched in, Cheesemite asked Rio: 'When can we get back to the old *Avenger*?'

'Very soon! Rio, he had enough of the land! He wanna get back to the sea, pronto, and the capitano, he wanna take our princess home; but she'll not want to stay, I bet!'

'I hope not. She's our princess an' she brings us luck. She'll not want to go back to her island, not after all she's done!' Tamina overheard and smiled to herself. She wanted to see her father again. But she was one of the buccaneers now and so she would remain!

To the joyous clamour of bells, the victorious army entered the Great Cathedral Square, where cheering crowds pressed round them. Suddenly, Roamer lost sight of the king. He gripped Tamina's paw. 'Where's Caladon?'

'Over on the far side of the square, talking to the cardinal. Do stop worrying, Roamer. Look – the city-mice are hauling him onto their shoulders! Oh, what a fabulous homecoming! Let's have another feast tonight; we'll buy some goodies in the market and take them to the orphans' house; they can celebrate with us, and we'll invite Matthias and Mother Bibo and – oh, everyone! Then it's back to the *Avenger*, and –'

Suddenly, a shot rang out. Tamina screamed. Caladon fell, blood streaming from his chest. Roamer swung round. *Where had the shot come from?* He stared up at the cathedral belltower. A whisp of smoke was curling from a high window.

'*Come on*!' The buccaneers crowding after him, Roamer pushed through the thunder-struck mice, flung open the cathedral door and dashed up the spiral staircase. The bells still pealed but as Roamer reached the little open space below the tower, the joyful clanging stopped abruptly. In the sudden silence, Roamer heard the creaking of a door behind him. He flung himself flat as a bullet zinged overhead and whined off the stone wall. 'Stay there!' he snapped as his buccaneers came tumbling up the stairs. Roamer drew his pistol and pushed open the door.

A narrow platform ended in a railing. Beyond, stretched the great wooden beam that ran the whole length of the cathedral. Halfway along, where a cluster of narrow timbers arched towards the distant rafters, was Flambeau. He was clutching a rifle and, as Roamer vaulted the railing and landed on the beam, the Red Duke glared at him and Roamer saw the madness in his eyes.

Roamer suddenly remembered that his pistol was unloaded. Cursing himself for his stupidity, he drew his cutlass and stepped out along the beam. Flambeau was ramming fresh powder into his rifle. Roamer would have to reach him before the gun was ready to fire.

Though Roamer was used to climbing to the dizzy heights of the *Avenger*'s masthead, there was always a rope or a section of rigging to cling to. But here, the yawning emptiness beneath him and the high, arching space above turned his legs to stone. He was sweating with fear. Unable to move, he watched as Flambeau spat a bullet into the gun barrel and rammed it home.

'Go on, Capitano!' hissed Rio from the doorway.

'Duck down, zur!' cried Ben. 'We'll give 'im a broadside!'

Roamer pulled himself together. 'Leave him to me.' He took a step forward, then another, his eyes fixed on the Red Duke.

'You've interfered for the last time, Roamer!' screamed Flambeau. 'I should have killed you long ago! Now I'm going to!' He clawed back the hammer and brought the rifle to his shoulder.

Roamer dropped his cutlass and ran full-tilt. The Duke's rifle flamed and roared, but Roamer was already diving and as Flambeau drew his dagger, Roamer hurled him onto the beam.

Flambeau's dagger flashed down, but Roamer caught his paw, squeezing and twisting it with all his strength. The duke yelled in pain, dropped the dagger and wrenched himself sideways. The buccaneers gasped as the two mice rolled to the very edge. The whole cathedral seemed to spin as Roamer tried desperately to dig his claws into the beam; but the ancient timber was hard as rock, Roamer's claws slithered off it and he fell.

Like an arrow, Hyperion streaked through the doors and up the aisle. In mid-air, Roamer made a wild grab for the eagle's talons. His paws were slippery with sweat but he clung on and Hyperion swooped to a graceful landing inches away from the high altar.

Marengo scrambled down from Hyperion's back and helped the shaken Roamer to his feet. 'Are you all right?'

Roamer was trembling. Never had he come so close to death. He smiled weakly at Marengo. 'Yes, thanks to you and Hyperion.'

'Thanks to the princess, you mean. She was

terrified that something dreadful was happening to you and begged me to come and take a look. Lucky I did.'

'What about Flambeau?' asked Roamer.

Marengo pointed down the aisle to where a body lay huddled on the stone floor. 'Dead. We're well rid of him. But I fear he's killed the king.'

The sound of weeping filled the square. Cranberry, Spital and Chowdmouse knelt beside Caladon, silently begging him not to die. Cardinal Matthias was praying deperately for the king's life. But Caladon was mortally wounded. Tamina was doing all she could. But not even her skill could save him.

A shadow fell over the dying king as Hyperion landed beside him. The great eagle was holding something in his beak. It was the ruby, which he had taken from the cathedral. Lowering his head, he gently placed the glowing jewel on Caladon's heart. The mice watched in awe as the ruby glowed ever brighter until the king's body was gently enfolded in rippling waves of light.

'Look!' whispered Tamina. A cloud had floated in front of the sun and the Great Star of the Lord of Light was shining brightly. Suddenly, a starbeam lanced down. It blended with the ruby's healing light and the mice caught their breath as a tremor passed through Caladon's body.

Scarcely daring to hope, Tamina reached out and touched Caladon's paw. 'He was cold,' she whispered. 'But now he's warm again.'

Caladon's searing pain died away and he felt his strength slowly returning. He raised his paw and grasped the ruby. Opening his eyes, he smiled at his friends.

'Roamer was right. I should have kept it. But I'll never let it go again.'

For a while longer, the Great Star shed its light over the grateful mice gathered in the square. Then, as the cloud passed, and the sun shone once more, the star faded until it was dim and pale in the summer sky.